Falling in Love at 40

by Lisa M Billingham

WARNING

This book contains scenes of a sexual nature.

This book may inspire you to follow your dreams.

First published in the UK in 2024

Copyright © 2024 by Lisa M Billingham

ALL RIGHTS RESERVED

ISBN: 978-1-8382929-4-2 (Paperback)
ISBN: 978-1-8382929-5-9 (eBook)

Dedication

This book is dedicated to my family, friends and followers who have supported me on my writing journey.

Some of the professional contacts used on this journey are available at the back of this book.

Sunday 6th November 2022 - Morning

Forty years and one day old Laurel feels like a wallflower. She rolls over on her double bed and stares at the space next to her. It has been years since the space had been filled, and her disaster of a birthday party last night has cemented her decision to find a new man. She knows she's ready. But where to look?

She grabs her ridiculously old Samsung mobile from the small chest of drawers at the side of the bed. Switching it on, she stares expectantly at the screen.

Nothing. Nada. No messages, no calls, not even a new notification from social media. Propping herself up on all four pillows Laurel logs into her Instagram account. Clicking the 'search' button, she types 'dating sites.' Pages and pages of accounts glare at her from the screen, 'follow me, follow me,' they appear to be calling to her. Laurel follows the top three and clicks on the first one to find their website details and register.

Oh, well. She sighs. *Welcome to the modern world of internet dating.*

Before she can click off Instagram a strange advert pops up:

Comedy Classic

Enter here to win two tickets to Parker Small's pre tour show. Winning tickets are for the evening of Thursday 17th November 2022 and include backstage passes.

Click the link in the comments to enter.

Who the devil is Parker Small? Laurel mutters. *And what damn silly algorithm has thrown a comedy show up in my feed? I've never been to one in my life.* Shaking her head, curiosity gets the better of her, and she clicks on the link. *What are you doing, woman?* She groans as she reads through the terms and conditions. She's shocked to learn that she knows the venue. She sings there once a month. *Ah,* she laughs, *so that's what the pesky algorithm picked up then. I follow the venue. I wonder why I haven't seen any posters for this show there. Invitation only, maybe?* She ponders.

Knowing the venue seals the deal for her as she knows they wouldn't scam anyone. *And you never know, it could be a good night.* Shrugging, she reads on for the competition entry details, *maybe I can buy tickets if I don't win.*

To enter submit a piece of writing which will make the judges laugh. It can be a song, poem, short story, limerick, or flash fiction, but:

- It must be less than 500 words,
- It must make the judges laugh,
- You must be available on the 17th November (19:30 – 21:30)
- You must like and share our page and comment on this post.

Laurel rolls her eyes at the like, comment, and share part. *Typically, algorithmy*, she tuts.

Saving the page and doing as she's been instructed; she likes and follows everything. Planning to write the piece later that afternoon, she goes back to the dating site she'd been looking at before being distracted.

Taking a deep breath, she begins setting up a new account. Of course, they want to know everything including her inside leg measurement. Once she's finished, she checks the time on her phone. 11:15. *Blimey, I'd better get going if I'm going to meet Kimberly for lunch*. Diving out of bed, her phone, the competition, and the dating site forgotten, she races to the shower. Dropping the towel a few minutes later, she dabs on a little deodorant. Pulling on her jeans and jumper, she grabs her car keys and races to her local park to meet her friend.

"Hey, Kimberly." She calls out as she spots her friend at one of the outdoor tables, making the most of the sunny day. Kimberly's head is bowed as she types on her phone.

Feeling around in her bag, *Oh, bother. I left mine on the bed*. Laurel curses as she wanders over to her friend to ask her what she fancies to eat. Scribbling their order on a tissue, so she doesn't forget it, she enters the coffee shop snuggled in the corner of the park to place their order.

Ambling back to her friend, table number in hand, Laurel sits down heavily on the bench opposite her rocking the table as she lands.

"Hey, Laurel, what's up?" Kimberly asks. "You look sad. Life begins at 40, don't you know?"

"Ha, it's alright for you, Kim, you're miles away from 40."

"I'm not, Lol, I'm 40 next year."

"See. Miles away." Laurel waves her hand in the air and they both burst out laughing.

"So, what have you been up to, Lol?" Kimberly asks, placing her phone in her bag so she could be 'in the moment' with her friend.

"Oh, not much. I registered with an online dating agency this morning."

"Ah, that's why you're looking flushed then, you've got yourself a date."

"Nah. I forgot to pick my phone up, so I don't know whether I've even got any messages."

"Are you kidding, Lol, a stunning lady like you, all long fiery red hair and a body to die for! You're bound to get loads of messages."

Laurel shrugs. "Yeah, well, I'll let you know. I just hope they're different to the last one. I don't think I can go through the heartache again."

"You won't. You're different now so you'll attract a good one this time."

"Mmm, I hope so," Laurel answers. "Ooh, I almost forgot, I'm going to enter a competition to see Parker Small's live preview show… Or something like that.

"Or something like that! Laurel, do you even know who he is?"

"Erm, nope, never heard of him."

"Oh. My. Word. Laurel Sage Rivers, where have you been hiding? He's hilarious, and he's a bit of a dish."

Laurel teases. "Is that all you think about, Kim?"

"Urm…no, not really…" Kim looks at her with an innocent face. They both burst out laughing knowing that really is all Kimberly thinks about.

"Are you sure you've never heard of him?" Kimberly asks as she digs her phone out of her bag to search for a picture of him.

Laurel, taking a sip of her drink which had just been delivered to the table, shook her head. "Nope. Never heard of him until that ad popped up on Insta."

"Oh, my gosh, Lol, is it genuine?"

"Yeah. It's where I work every month, Hattie's, in town. I know they're straight."

"Oh, cool, I love that venue. I'm so excited. I'm coming with you when you win." Kimberly can barely contain her excitement.

"I have to win first, Kim." Laurel giggles. Thriving on Kim's positivity.

"Ah, you will. It's just a follow, like, share thing I bet."

"No, actually they're making you work for it. You have to write something."

"Ooh, well, that's easy for you, Miss singer-songwriter extraordinaire." Kimberly is Laurel's number one fan. Has been ever since she took to the stage. She is always positive and encouraging. Even in Laurel's darkest times Kimberly never stopped believing that Laurel would make the big time.

"Ha, ha, very funny. I have one gig a month there and one every three months up the road." Laurel sighs.

"At the moment. That doesn't mean it will be like that forever. You have to believe in yourself, Lol. You know it will happen. When the timing is right."

Laurel nods her head, finishing her drink. Grateful that she has such a good friend in Kimberly.

Later That Day

Laurel's thumbs are tired from scrolling through the ridiculous number of likes and messages she's received. She's only been gone for a couple of hours, but it would take a couple more to go through the messages from the dating app. *Oh, my goodness,* she groans, *can't you guys think of anything more exciting to write apart from 'hi there?'*

Shaking her head she sits on her bed, legs crossed beneath her, her body moaning at the strange angle it finds itself at. After a while, Laurel finally whittles it down to three possible men who may be dating material. Sick to death of one-night stands and empty promises. (She's even written that on her profile,) she takes a deep breath and sends them all a message. At least these had written; *'hi, there, how are you?'* That was progress.

Feeling better after her lunch with Kimberly, Laurel leaves her phone on the bed and grabs her music books from her bedside table. Her spare cupboard sized bedroom has all her equipment set up. She heads there to rehearse the songs for the wedding she is singing at later that month.

Spending the afternoon practicing, she had almost forgotten the dating app. Taking a break to rest her voice, she grabs her phone from her bedroom and scrolls through her notifications. After answering a few queries for singing appearances she turns her attention to the dating app. She spots a red heart against one of the messages she'd sent. Opening the message, she clicks on the profile. He's responded to her message. *Mmm, this looks promising.*

Hi Laurel my name is Ricardo I really like your profile as I'm into travel, singing and reading too. Can we connect please?

Well heeellllooo, Ricardo, Laurel giggles. Looking at his profile picture she could see herself curling up in his arms with a good book. "Oh well, here goes nothing," she calls out into thin air.

Hi Ricardo, I'd love to connect, where have you been travelling?

Within seconds she receives a reply.

Oh, everywhere. I've lived on all seven continents but I'm currently back in the UK. How about u?

Laurel takes a break from texting to cook herself her favourite dinner, Spaghetti Bolognese. She's feeling good. Her singing voice is getting stronger with every practice session. She's confident one of the enquiries she received earlier will come off and she's texting a nice young man. What more could a woman want? Back on her phone, Laurel responds.

Wow, that's some travelling, I've only been to Europe, but I've visited Spain, Italy, and Germany. Seems I need to get my finger out to catch up with you.

Again, the reply is there within seconds, leaving Laurel wondering whether it was an algorithm, or a person behind the messages.

14

Saturday 12th November 2022

"I'm so nervous, Kim," Laurel squeals down the phone at her best friend. "What if..."

"Lol, you do this every time. Stop getting your knickers in a twist and enjoy the date. It's your first one for three years, you're bound to be nervous. Text me when you get there and when you get back. And, more importantly, if you need to get out of there. Make sure there are a few people in the coffee shop before you go in though."

Laurel is smiling to herself, I'm so lucky to have a friend like Kim. Always has my back.

"I will, Kim, I promise. I'd better go or else I'll be late."

"Keep him waiting, won't hurt him."

Laurel is never late. She prides herself on being early for everything. Dressing in a pair of casual trousers and a loose-fitting blouse, she ties her long red hair into a ponytail and heads off. Excitement flutters in her belly.

Ricardo had already told her he'd be wearing bike riding gear as he was planning to ride over.

As she locks the car, she spots a bicycle tied to the lamppost on the main road. *That must be his. At least he's here. That's a good start.*

Walking past the flower beds, she enters the coffee shop. Apart from the staff there's only one man and one other couple there. *Oh blimey, I hope the couple don't leave and I'll be left here on my own with a stranger.* Girding her loins, Laurel walks over to the lone gentleman. "Are you Ricardo?"

"Yes, you must be Laurel, pleased to meet you." He rises to shake her hand.

A sense of trepidation claws at her stomach. He looks a little bit like his profile picture, but not much.

Sitting down, they order drinks, Laurel refuses food, feeling too sick to be able to enjoy it.

They fall into a strange silence whilst they wait for the drinks. *Odd*, she thinks. *He was talkative on the app.*

Fed up with the eerie silence, Laurel asks, "How are you?"

"Oh, erm, I'm good, thank you. How are you?"

"Yes, I'm good too, thank you."

"What do you do for a living, Laurel?" He asks.

"I'm a singer... And a receptionist. How about you?"

"I'm in... insurance."

The way he says the word insurance makes the hairs on Laurel's neck stand to attention. *Bloody hell, he sounds like a hitman*. Looking at the scar she's been trying to avoid noticing, she has a feeling he may well be one. "Oh, that's... interesting."

Laurel's stomach is churning. She's never normally stuck for words, but she feels uncomfortable. Making her excuses, she finds the bathroom and ponders what to do. *I have to leave. This does not feel good.*

For once listening to her intuition, she slides out of the bathroom. Where their table is would make it impossible for him to see her. Glancing over at Ricardo, he is engrossed in something on the table. She heads to the door. Thankfully she makes it to her car without being seen. Not wanting him to suspect anything or see her number plate, she races off the car park and heads for home. Her heart in her mouth. *I have to delete that bloody app*. She curses as she pulls up in her parking space.

through Mike, but that's a story for another day." Parker doesn't like talking about himself, so he turns back to her. "What are your dreams, Laurel?" Parker asks as their food arrives.

Grateful for the break to gather her thoughts, Laurel starts her breakfast. "Mmm, one of them is to appear on a big stage. But I'm quite shy and I get a bit overwhelmed by large crowds."

Laurel looks up from her plate to see Parker grinning from ear to ear.

"Hey, what's funny?" She questions, popping more hash brown into her mouth.

"You. You make me smile. It's okay to be shy and to be on stage you know."

"Yes, I know. My friends find it hilarious. It's like I lose myself up there. It's almost like I'm acting a part and it's not really me. Does that make any sense at all?" Laurel looks back down at her food, feeling silly telling a stranger her innermost secrets.

Parker is wolfing down his breakfast but stops to look into Laurel's eyes. "It makes perfect sense to me. I'm the same."

"Are you? Really? You don't come across like that on the stage."

He smiles again. "I must be doing it right then."

Laurel smiles back, "Yes, you must be."

All too soon their breakfast is finished, and their date is nearly over. Laurel feels the chemistry as he grabs her hand and leads her out onto the street once he's paid the bill. Her brain is telling her to stay away. He's bound to be a player with the job he does, but her heart tells her something altogether different. She can't believe he's going away for six months.

31

Parker walks Laurel back to her car, kissing her on the cheek to say goodbye. "Please keep in touch while I'm away." Parker's eyes plead with her as he moves to kiss her lips, but he moves away, aware that kissing her would be unfair.

"I will." She promises as she gets in her car and winds the window down. "Keep in touch too and stay safe."

Parker kisses her forehead as she starts the engine then stands back and waves her off the car park. Rooted to the spot, he can't believe he's just met this gorgeous lady and now he's going to be away for half a year. *I have to make the effort to keep in touch with this one.* He promises himself as he calls a taxi to take him to the airport.

Parker tells her everything that's been happening while he's been away and asks if they can do a video call one of the days when neither of them is working. It proves a little difficult to get the timings right, but they agree to the following Saturday morning.

"I need to go, Parker, I'm sorry, I have to get ready for my singing coach."

"Okay, I have to get ready for tonight's show too."

They put the phone down, both missing the other already.

The Zoom Call – The Following Saturday Morning 26th November 2022

Laurel can barely contain her excitement this morning. Only 2 hours before she gets to video call Parker. To keep her mind occupied, she cleans the flat. Twice. Always an early riser she was up even earlier today. Excitement made it almost impossible to sleep last night.

Laurel has on her favourite black dress, chosen especially for her 'date.' Her red hair, trimmed yesterday, is hanging loose around her smiling face. Only 1 hour 59 minutes to go. *Oh, come on Laurel, get a grip, woman*, she curses herself as she heads to her spare bedroom. Practising her set for the wedding she is singing at next week will help her focus.

7am on the dot she hears her laptop ding to signify a video call coming in. *Wow, he's keen*, Laurel smiles to herself. *Makes a nice change.*

Sitting at her tidy but compact desk Laurel accepts the call.

"It's so good to see you, Laurel," Parker is first to speak. *She looks gorgeous*, he thinks to himself. Even more stunning than he remembers.

"It's good to see you too, Parker," Laurel responds. Dying to say, I miss you so much, but manages, for once, to keep the thought to herself. "How's your tour going?"

"It's going well, thank you. I've got a few ideas for the next one. Very different from this one, but I need to run them by my brother first."

"That sounds exciting, what are your ideas?"

"Ooh, I don't know whether I should share them, yet." Parker teases.

Laurel stares at the screen, unable to judge whether he's being cagey, or he wants to give the ideas some more thought. *He barely knows me, why should he trust me with his ideas.*

Sensing her disquiet, Parker interrupts her thoughts. "I will tell you, Laurel. I just need to get it straight in my head first."

"Oh, okay, thank you," Laurel stutters, *maybe he's a mind reader as well as a comedian.*

"Now, Laurel, I have some good news."

"Really, what is it?" Barely able to contain her excitement, hoping he'll say he's coming home early; he shocks her into the middle of next week.

"Yes, I think you'll like it. I've been looking at your social media accounts."

Laurel racks her brains. *Oh, hell, is there anything on there I should have taken down?* She ponders as Parker continues talking.

"So, what do you say, can I introduce you to my brother?"

Why on earth is he trying to farm me off to his brother? Doesn't he fancy me?

"Laurel." Parker calls. "Laurel, did you hear me?"

Thinking on her feet, Laurel responds, "Oh, sorry, I think the signal broke up then; what did you say?"

"My brother knows a few people in the music industry, and I've shown him the video of you from your last gig at Hattie's. He wants to talk to you. He thinks his contacts can help you."

Laurel stares dumbfounded at the screen. *Did I hear him correctly?*

46

"What do you say, Laurel? I know I'm biased, as he's my brother, but he's good at his job."

Stuttering and still in shock, Laurel finally answers, "Wow, thank you so much, that would be great. I'd love to speak to him."

Parker's shoulders relax. The look on her face at first causing him to wonder if he's done the right thing. He knows he has. He can help her, and he wants to. He wants to see her succeed. Strange as they've only just met, but their connection is strong, and something he's never experienced before. "I'll give him your number and get him to contact you. It might take him a while, he's busy bossing me around at the moment." Parker laughs.

Still in shock, Laurel mumbles, "Okay, thank you so much."

"Now, what have you been up to?" Parker asks.

Laurel so wants to hear about him, his tour, and his ideas for his next tour, but it seems she's not going to find out much more today. She fills him in on her practice for the wedding and confirms she's made the right decision in resigning from her reception job. If she hadn't, Parker wouldn't have suggested speaking to his brother, would he?

It doesn't take long to fill him in on her life, so she asks about his tour. He's enjoying it by the animated way he's talking about it and Laurel can't help but feel a little jealous. *Why can't I have what he's got?* Laurel muses. *Stop it, woman. Life is good, just go with it and speak to Parker's brother.*

An hour and a half later, all caught up, they are interrupted by a knock on Parker's door.

"Sorry, Laurel, I have to go, that will be Brian. We're moving further north today so we have to leave to set up for tonight."

47

Disappointed but understanding, Laurel nods.

"Bye, Laurel, I'll be in touch soon."

"Bye, Parker." Is left hanging in the air as the screen goes blank.

Laurel sits back in her chair. Mixed emotions flood her veins. Missing him terribly, happy that he's happy, and curious about what Brian may say. Determined to keep busy, she switches her laptop off and goes back to her singing. Her emotions clearly showing in her voice.

Two days later - 28th November 2022

Laurel is shocked into wakefulness by the incessant ringing of her phone. As if the sound isn't loud enough, the vibration through her bedside table hammers through her skull. Sorely tempted to knock it off its perch, she reaches her arm out of bed and pulls the phone under the quilt. One eye half open she stares at the strange number then clocks the time. "4am," she squeals. "Who the hell is calling me at 4am?" A thought occurs to her. *Oh, my, Parker. I hope he's okay.* Sitting up quicker than she would have liked. Her skull seems to rattle around her brain before she presses what she thinks is the green button and croaks, "Hello, who is this?"

"Ah, Laurel, I presume. At last."

"Er, yes, this is Laurel." Her heart beats faster as the stranger continues talking. The voice seems familiar, but she can't place it.

"… sorry to call so early but we have a full-on week this week and Parker insisted I call you today."

Ah. Brian. Parker's brother. The penny drops as Laurel staggers out of bed to make herself a strong coffee. She needs to be alert for this potentially life-changing call.

Stirring her coffee, Laurel listens intently to Brian. "I've watched your latest video several times, and I think, no… I know… you're just what my music industry buddies are looking for. You have the voice of an angel.

Laurel is stunned. "Th…thank you," she mutters.

"I'll connect you with my contact. She's a bit wild, but you'll love her. Any questions?"

So many questions pop into Laurel's head but she can't seem to articulate them into words.

Brian laughs, "You've gone quiet, Laurel, are you okay?"

"Yes… erm...I'm fine, thank you so much."

"You sound a bit nonplussed, are you sure you're okay?"

Always honest, which is sometimes her downfall, Laurel responds. "I am a little. This feels like a dream come true but... I…I don't think I can do it..." The doubting of her abilities, which she's had since she was a child, raise their ugly head.

"You can, Laurel. Believe in yourself. Parker is wearing your video out he's watching it so often, and he's telling everyone about it too. He believes in you. I believe in you. Now you need to believe in you."

"But... Parker barely knows me, and you don't know me at all." It all seems too good to be true to Laurel, but she knows she has asked the universe to help her so maybe...just maybe... this is her universal angel.

"I know a sensation when I see one, Laurel. And on that note, I have to go. I've just sent you Petra's contact details. Please call her, she's waiting to speak to you. She's based in London so maybe give her an hour or so to get up." At that he laughs and bids Laurel farewell, promising to contact her the following week for an update.

I hope he doesn't ring so early next week, is the final thought Laurel has before her emotions get the better of her. Tears of joy fall down her cheeks as she pinches herself to see if this is all a dream.

It isn't.

The Following Day

The following day, during a gruelling all-day singing practice session, the shrill of the phone brings Laurel back to earth. "Hello." She tentatively answers, not recognising the number.

"Hey, Laurel, baby, is that you, girl?" The strange high-pitched voice asks.

"Erm, yes, this is Laurel."

"I caught you. Good. It's Petra returning your calls. Sorry I missed you yesterday. Can you come to London tomorrow to see me?"

Things seem to be moving a little too quickly for Laurel, she can barely take a breath before Petra pipes up.

"Please say you will, I'm dying to meet you."

"Yes of course I will."

"Wonderful, darling, my secretary will send you the details if you ping your email address to this number."

Before Laurel can say thank you, the line goes dead. "Thank you," she calls out and looks skywards. *Thank you, angels.*

Sending her details as requested, Laurel waits nervously for the email notification to sound on her phone. She sits on the bed staring at the screen for half an hour before she shakes herself and continues her practice. *Come on, girl,* she mumbles to herself, *watching the phone isn't going to make it ping.*

A couple of hours later she stops for her evening meal and checks her notifications. Sure enough, there it is, the email that could change her life. With a slight sense of trepidation, she opens it and reads the instructions. Simple enough but blimey, flipping early start.

She grabs a light meal and an early night ready for tomorrow.

Whirlwind Interview

Laurel gets comfy in her seat on the train and settles back to read her book. The 2-hour journey flies by in a puff of smoke.

Before she knows it, she's standing in the reception area of Petra's offices. Painted garishly but with a strangely welcoming feeling, Laurel gazes around and admires the paintings on the wall. All landscape art, but they match the decor perfectly. No nerves attack Laurel like they usually do. She feels at home here. Like she's been here before. *Mmm, maybe in a dream.* She ponders to herself as a whirlwind of a bundle of fun, which she assumes is Petra, bounces through the door, and grabs her in a massive bear hug.

"Hey, Laurel, I recognised you from your video, follow me." Petra gushes as she beckons Laurel through the door to their left. "Take a seat, take a seat," Petra waves enthusiastically at Laurel and beckons her to sit on the fluffy sofa.

Laurel sits, well, falls into the seat as it envelops her in a hug. She feels comfortable here. Safe.

Petra laughs as Laurel's legs tip up in the air as she lands on the seat. *Mmm, nice knickers,* Petra mumbles under her breath. She sits at the opposite end of the L-shaped sofa, and eyes Laurel up and down.

Laurel catches her eye and smiles, unsure how to start the conversation.

"So, Laurel, I've watched your latest amateur video, and I have to say, it's really rather good. I see gazillions of the things and they're usually shite, but yours is good. It shows you're serious about your career. Where do you see yourself in 3 years?"

53

Laurel groans inwardly, *how many bloody times have I heard that before.* Without thinking twice she blurts out, "performing on the biggest stage in the UK to a full house."

Petra stares at her and nods. "That's a good start, Lol, may I call you Lol?"

"Erm, thank you, and yes, most of my friends call me Lol."

"That's good. I think you and I will become very good friends. So, how do you know the demi-god we call Brian? Not that he floats my boat, if you know what I mean?" Petra winks but Laurel misses it.

It takes Laurel a few seconds for her brain to engage. "Oh, I know him through his brother, Parker. We met just before he started his tour."

Petra raises her eyebrow. "Wow. It usually takes Parker a few years before he introduces potential superstars to me. You must be very special, young lady."

Laurel is lost for words, unusual for her but this all seems so... surreal.

Grabbing her notepad and pen from the table in front of her, Petra asks Laurel more questions. "Why the biggest stage in the UK? Why not the biggest stage in the world?"

Laurel stares open-mouthed. "Well, er, I have to start somewhere." Was all Laurel could think of in reply.

Still nodding, Petra continues with the questions. When they finish, an hour and a half later, Petra holds out her hand. "Welcome to the agency. We'll be seeing you on the biggest stage in the world."

Laurel beams from ear to ear and shakes Petra's hand. "Thank you so much."

She leaves Petra's office walking on cloud nine. *Oh, my days*. So much has happened in such a short time. She heads towards the station coffee shop to gather her thoughts before she catches the train home. *The universe is certainly sending me a few angels.*

Call With Parker - A Few Days Later

Laurel's feet barely touch the floor following her meeting with Petra. Email after email of all the plans Petra wants to put in place for her. Laurel loves Petra's energy but, boy oh boy she's like a machine. Putting her phone on silent she concentrates on writing a new song which has been floating around her head for days. She is shocked when she picks it up a couple of hours later to find three missed calls from Parker. *Oh, my word. I hope he's okay.* She thinks as she tries but fails to return the call. Checking the time, 7pm. *Oh, bother.* She curses under her breath; he'll be getting ready to go on stage.

Upset that she's missed him she grabs a drink and snack from the kitchen and curls her feet underneath her on the sofa, settling down to wait for his return call. Around 1am her eyes lose the battle, and she dozes into a fitful sleep, her dreams flashing all kinds of scenarios in her subconscious brain.

At 5am she is awoken from her slumber by the ringing of her phone. Her heart races as she checks the number and answers. "Parker, are you okay? I'm so sorry I missed your calls."

Parker laughs, "I'm fine thank you. Stop panicking. I just wanted to see how you got on with Petra. Brian says the meeting went well."

"Yes, it did. Better than I could ever have imagined. Thank you so much for introducing me and thank your brother for me too. This is life changing."

Smiling to himself, *I kind of thought it would be.* He responds. "You're welcome. Tell me all about it."

Laurel gushes the words out and tells him everything. She's never felt excitement like it.

"I'm scared though, Parker. Petra has high hopes for me. What if I screw it up?" Finally, Laurel takes a breath and Parker answers.

"Laurel, it's all new to you. Stay calm, keep focused and positive and you'll smash it."

"You're there. You're at the height of success, and you've achieved your dreams. What is it like?"

Parker, like Laurel, is always honest to a fault. He doesn't believe in lying or sugar coating anything.

"It's hard work, Laurel. But worth it."

Laurel's shoulders sag and Parker can feel it all those miles away. "I can't work much harder, Parker. I'm knackered as it is."

"I know how you feel. Everything you've done up to this point has been worth it. Even if you don't think it has. It's got you here. It's got you the contacts. Don't give up."

"Are you reading my mind, or something, Parker?" Laurel asks. Feeling like she wants to hibernate for a hundred years and come out when it's all over.

"I've been there. It's still hard work, even now but I enjoy it. That's the main thing. And you will too."

Laurel is grateful for Parker's positivity but the self-doubt niggles away in the back of her mind. Sighing, "I know you're right, Parker. I just don't know whether superstardom is for me."

Oh, it is, girl. It is. Parker knows it is, but he also knows how hard the transition is from relative pauper to superstar.

"Take it a day at a time, Laurel. Petra will help you, that's what she's there for. And you've got Brian and me too."

"But you barely know me."

"I know enough."

Mmm, Laurel murmurs to herself as a pleasant silence descends between the miles.

"Enough about me." Laurel is the first to break it. "How is your tour going?" She asks. Dying to add, I miss you, to the conversation but not daring to for fear of rejection or ridicule. Or both.

"Oh, it's okay."

"Just okay? I thought you loved your work. Doesn't sound like it right now."

"I do… I… Just… miss you." *There I said it.* Parker surprises himself.

"I miss you too, Parker. It doesn't make sense, does it? We barely know each other."

"I know. I must admit it's a new experience for me, but there is something about you, Laurel. You're gorgeous, clever, sexy as hell and I want to see you."

Laurel swallows the lump in her throat. Not used to compliments from handsome men, she is taken aback.

"When does your tour finish?"

"Not for another 5 months or more."

They both sigh, "Maybe I could come and visit you. You know, when you have a few dates in one area?" Laurel tentatively asks. Not wishing to appear desperate or too forward but wanting to see him so badly it hurts.

"I'd love that, Laurel. I'll get one of the girls to send you the itinerary, and let's see if we can work something out. Now you're on your way to superstardom yourself you may not have time for little old me." Parker says, feeling a little trepidation as he knows she will be busy recording with Petra for a few weeks.

"Okay," Laurel answers, "I hope we can work something out. It will be great to see you again. Maybe we can do another video call in the meantime?"

"Yes, I'd like that," Parker responds, checking his diary. Keen to get a date sorted now.

Recording Session with Petra - Tuesday 20th December 2022

Laurel's head hasn't stopped spinning since she signed with Petra's agency. She is exhausted and looking forward to Christmas so she can put her feet up and catch up on some sleep. She's barely spoken to Parker and the text messages seem to be getting fewer and farther between. She's worried.

Petra pushes the button on the console in front of her to communicate with Laurel in the singing booth. "That's a wrap, as they say in the industry."

Oh, thank God. Laurel almost cries. Her body visibly relaxes. She's grateful that she can finally go home and rest.

Dragging her weary body into her bedroom, Laurel falls flat on her back onto the bed. Not bothering to get undressed, it's almost midnight and her body is crying out for sleep. Within seconds she is snoring gently and dreaming of her future.

His muscular body hovers over her as she lies dozing on the 3-seater settee. The pillow is plump beneath her head, and her hand is tucked underneath. She is naked. He stares down at her.

"My sleeping beauty," he mutters under his breath. It is the middle of the night and she's stayed up late waiting for him to return from his world tour. The

large print thriller she's been reading lies forlornly by her side, forgotten as it slipped out of her hand. He picks the book up and places it silently on the large glass-topped coffee table. He's been waiting for this moment for 6 months. He hasn't the heart to wake her, she's just finished a tour herself and only arrived home a few hours earlier.

Parker is a gentle giant. His olive skin glistens in the glow of the moonlight chinking through the gap in the blinds. He's never felt love quite like the love he feels for Laurel. She is his rock. Parker kneels on the floor next to her, stroking the side of her face. To Laurel it feels like a feather tickling her skin, to Parker it feels like a bolt of electricity. The urge to wake her growing stronger by the second, he wants to take this girl in his arms and hold her. Forever.

Laurel stirs slightly, the tickle instigates a swipe of her hand as she, half dozing now, tries to brush it away. "Mmm," she purrs as the tickle continues. Her eyes flicker as she stretches out to her full 5'3" frame. Yawning it takes her a second to realise the tickle is still there. Opening her eyes, she sees Parker's beautiful brown eyes staring lovingly into hers.

"Oh, babe, you're back." She sits up and flings her arms around Parker's muscular neck. "I missed you so much. How long have you been sitting there?"

"Only a few minutes. But it feels like days. You looked so peaceful; I didn't want to wake you."

Laurel stands so she can hug him properly. Parker slides his hands around her waist and pulls her into his body. Relaxing into each other's arms, they cling to each other like their lives depend on it.

After a few moments, Parker stands back and holds her away from him. "Let me drink you in, babe, I missed you so much."

Her baby blue eyes stare into his, nothing else matters in that moment. They're safe, they're together, they're happy. They lean forward, he looks down as she looks up and their lips meet. They both close their eyes as the kiss, gentle at first, intensifies. His tongue finds hers and they play. Lost in that moment their souls connect. They are one. The heat of their desire and love for each other deepens as the kiss deepens. 6 months of burning desire erupts in that one kiss.

Parker wraps his arms around her slender body and picks her up, his lips never leaving hers. Carrying her to the bedroom, he lays her gently on the king-size four poster bed. Their lips part as they catch their breath. Staring down at her, he takes her right nipple into his mouth and nibbles. Her body rises off the bed, desperate for his. She pulls him closer to her. Deftly undoing his belt, she releases his throbbing penis from its zipped cage. Gently, she toys with it. Running her fingers expertly up and down the shaft.

"Argh," he cries. "Careful, don't make me cum too quickly, babe."

Slowing the pace, Laurel wriggles from his grasp, her nipple fully erect and so sensitive she feels like she's going to explode. Pulling him onto the bed, she *deftly rolls him onto his back. Her hands grip his hands, and she pushes them over his head. She slides her body along his until she finds his penis and expertly slides herself onto it. Each movement sends shock waves through their bodies. Fully connected they move together, gently at first. Staring into each other's eyes again they find their rhythm and within a matter of moments, the earth-shattering orgasm engulfs them both.*

Wednesday 21ˢᵗ December 2022

What the hell is that? Laurel sits bolt upright as the shrill of a phone disturbs her dream. The dream felt so real, Laurel looks around for Parker. *Wow.* She thinks. *I wonder if that's a sign of what's to come.* The beginnings of a headache form in the recess of her brain as the incessant ringing continues. Laurel searches the bedclothes, the chest of drawers, and the floor for her phone. *Where is the blasted thing?* Scratching her head, she realises, as she's still fully clothed, she must have left it in her bag. Scratting around on her hands and knees she finds the bag, obviously slung under the bed in haste last night, and pulls her phone out. Her heart skips a beat. "Hi, Parker."

"Hi, Laurel, I'm sorry. Did I wake you?"

Laurel squints at her phone. 6am. Still feeling dozy, she answers, "erm, yeah, late one at the studio but it's all done." Relief and exhilaration take over her body as she sits back down on the edge of her double bed. She pinches herself. "Parker. I just recorded an album. Oh. My. God." Laurel rambles. Parker waits for her to calm down. He can feel her excitement despite being hundreds of miles away.

"I'm so sorry, I'm rambling, aren't I? How are you?"

Laughing Parker answers, "I'm fine, I'm fine. I just finished my last gig for a few days. I don't perform now until boxing day. What are you doing over Christmas?"

"Ah, that's good. You can have a nice break. Not much, I haven't really thought about it I've been so busy. What are you doing? Are you coming home?" Laurel's voice begins to break. She prays he says yes so that she can see him again and they can talk properly.

"No, sadly, I'm not coming home."

Laurel is crestfallen. Her heart sinks to her feet, and as she fights back the tears, she almost misses his invitation.

"Sorry, Parker, what did you say?"

"Would you consider spending Christmas with me? In Scotland?"

"Wow. Really?" Laurel questions, uncertain whether she's heard him correctly.

"Yes, really. You could get the train up here."

Laurel's brain is in overdrive thinking of all the things she needs to do before she goes back into the studio in January. Her life has changed so much she's still catching up with herself. A break will do her good though.

"Oh, yes, I'd love to. I'll check the trains. Will they be running tomorrow?"

"Well, I was thinking, how about today?" Parker answers almost a statement rather than a question.

"Today?"

"Yes." He laughs. "Now, maybe?"

"Oh, my." Laurel is stunned.

"You said you don't have any plans so…why not?"

Smiling, Laurel banters. "Why not indeed. You only live once, and I like a bit of spontaneity."

"Excellent. Text me all the details of the train you will catch to Edinburgh Waverley, and I'll send you a ticket by email."

"You don't need to do that, Parker." Laurel isn't used to being treated to things and it comes as a bit of a shock.

"No, I don't, but I want to. Go and get packed and send me the details. I'll see you soon."

Without waiting for a response, Parker hangs up, unable to keep the huge grin off his face. *Finally, a girl who appreciates me.*

After checking the times and sending the information to Parker to book her tickets, Laurel races around like an idiot to pack her case. *Oh, my word, oh, my word, oh, my word.* She mutters to herself as she gets into the taxi. She's cutting it fine, and with the London traffic bound to affect her journey, she prays she makes it to the station on time.

She does. She breathes a sigh of relief as she takes her book out, pops her ear buds in, and settles in for the uneventful 5-hour journey.

"The train is now approaching Edinburgh Waverley. Please ensure you have all your belongings and take care when stepping from the train onto the platform edge." Blares over the tannoy. Laurel collects her things, excitement threatens to boil over, she is so looking forward to seeing Parker again. Although she's only met him a couple of times, she feels like she's known him forever. *Bizarre,* she thinks, but doesn't question it. No butterflies in the tummy prevail and she takes that as a good sign. All previous dates and relationships used to send the butterflies into overdrive. *And look how they turned out.* She thinks as she pulls the case down onto the platform. *Trust me to sit in the carriage furthest away from the exit.* She can't help but laugh. *The exercise will do me good.*

Totally oblivious to the world around her, she almost careers into a tall, butch man in a suit who is holding a piece of paper up with her name on it.

He recognises her from the music video his boss had shown him when he sent him to collect her. Knowing she wouldn't be looking for him, he tries to intercept her. This wasn't quite what he had in mind but at least he's found her.

"Oh, I'm so sorry," Laurel stammers, "are you hurt?" Laughing to herself at the ridiculous comment. It would take a bulldozer to hurt this gentle giant.

"I'm fine, Miss Laurel. Are you okay?" he asks. She looks rather shaken.

"Erm yes, yes, I'm fine, thank you. How...why...what?" She has so many questions, she doesn't know where to start. It feels like she's starring in a surreal movie. Things like this just don't happen to her.

To save her any further embarrassment, he introduces himself. "I'm Clifford. Parker's driver. He sent me to collect you, he's just finishing some paperwork with Brian so he can relax for a few days."

Laurel's shoulders visibly relax as she breathes a sigh of relief. "Ah. Okay. I wasn't expecting a lift, so this is a nice surprise, thank you very much."

Clifford takes her case from her and points towards the side exit to the station. "Come on, let's get you to the hotel."

Laurel follows him and stares as he opens the rear door of a pristine white stretch limousine. Her mouth falls open. Clifford waits for her to gather herself together, then dons his hat and takes his seat behind the wheel. He opens the dividing window and presses a button on the dashboard.

"Make yourself at home, we have an hour or so's journey. Help yourself to drinks, and if you need anything, press the little green button on the centre armrest."

Clifford closes the window, smiling to himself. He likes her. She's so different from all Parker's former girlfriends. Most of them made impossible demands, were rude and expected him to be at their beck and call, just like Parker was. She seems to be a genuinely nice girl. *Fingers crossed it works out for them.* Clifford ponders as he starts the engine and heads towards Stirling and the best spa hotel in the country.

Laurel takes in her plush surroundings. The space is bigger than her flat. She can't help wondering why he didn't send her to a closer train station. *Maybe there isn't one?*

Laurel takes her phone out of her bag when she feels it vibrate against her leg. She's so awe struck, she almost forgot she had one.

"Hello."

"Laurel, hi. Has Clifford picked you up yet?" Parker asks, his excitement palpable, even over the phone.

"Yes, he has. Thank you so much, Parker, I wasn't expecting all this."

"You're very welcome, Laurel. Have you ever ridden in a limo before?"

"No, never. It's like a home from home. I can't believe it. You didn't need to do all this."

"I wanted to, Laurel. It's been a long time since I've been able to spoil a lady." He answers. *This one is genuinely grateful.*

"I have so much planned for us while you're here. I hope you're ready to be swept off your feet."

Laurel laughs. *There's a first time for everything.* "I think I can cope with that." She responds.

"Sit back, relax, and enjoy the ride. I'll see you soon."

Laurel does exactly that. She gazes out of the window and watches the world go by. Some of the scenery takes her breath away. *Why have I never been here before. This place is beautiful.*

Before she knows it, Clifford is opening the door and helping her out. She comes face to face with a stunning castle like building. The atmosphere is calming, and she's looking forward to staying here.

"Laurel, Laurel, you made it." Parker dashes down the stairs and envelops her in the biggest, strongest bear hug she's ever experienced. She throws her arms around him and reciprocates.

"Wow, that was some hug, Laurel." It takes his breath away. This was not something he was used to either.

He grabs her hand, "come on, I'll show you to your room."

Laurel follows him, admiring his backside. (As you do.) They enter the lift, and he presses the penthouse button. *Blimey. I didn't know they had penthouses over here. I thought they were an American thing.*

The air in the lift is intoxicating. Laurel leans against the lift wall, not trusting herself to keep her hands off his muscular torso. Parker, his hands in his pockets, stares at the control panel, not trusting himself to keep his hands off her pert little bottom.

The ping of the lift doors opening brings them out of their reverie. Laurel steps into a room as big as a ballroom. The huge king-sized bed at the far end almost feels as if it's next door, it's so far away. The mahogany desk and 4-seater sofa complete the furniture in the room. The decor, although very old fashioned, lends a crisp, clean, and comfortable air to the room. She is mesmerized.

"You're boudoir, Madam." Parker says as he waves his arm around, welcoming her into the room.

Laurel gulps. "What do you mean? My boudoir."

"This is all yours. I'll be through that door there." He points to the door in the far-right corner. "Come on, I'll show you."

Through the door is an exact replica of the room.

"Oh, my." Laurel exclaims.

"Do you like your room?" Parker asks, concerned as Laurel hasn't said anything for a few minutes. He's not sure whether she's breathed in that time either.

"I love it. Thank you so much, you shouldn't have." She feels overwhelmed, and tears of joy spring to her eyes. *Thank you, Angels.* She says under her breath. She has been asking them to send her a good man, honest and true and she feels sure it's Parker. The treats are a nice bonus. Little does she know how much more extravagant those treats will become over the next few days.

Parker leaves her to get freshened up while he has a meeting with his brother.

Laurel stands still for a few moments, taking in her surroundings. *Wow.* Is all she can think. *Just. Wow.* Slowly getting undressed, she heads to the huge bathroom to take a nice hot bath. Everything aches. Even her fingernails. She pours a teaspoon full of the expensive looking bath crème into the shell shaped, pristine white bathtub and climbs in. The subtle scent of jasmine dances in her nostrils and she takes a deep breath to help her relax. Clearing her mind. She knows her life is changing, for the better, and she's finding it a little overwhelming.

At the side of the bath is what looks like a futuristic radio. She fiddles with the dials and finds the hotels own radio station. *This is exciting,* she mumbles, *I didn't know hotels had their own radio stations, how cute.*

The station is playing relaxing meditation music and Laurel allows her mind to wonder. All her senses are heightened, and her life plays out in front of her like an old black and white movie. Urging her to let go of the past, think big, and look towards the future.

Luxuriating in the bubbles, Laurel is sure she's dreaming. The first song on her newly recorded and, she thought, not yet released, debut album is blaring in her left ear. The sound of the internal phone beeping brings her round from her reverie. Opening her eyes, she reaches in front of her to pick up the handset of the diamanté studded phone. She pauses. My song is playing. My. Song. Is. Playing. On. The. Radio. *How the hell did that happen?* Her body flushes with emotions. Everything from fear to elation and back again. My. Song. Is. Playing. On. The. Radio. Oh. My. God.

The phone her fingertips are resting on is vibrating off the wall in its urgency to be answered. She picks it up.

"Laurel, finally. Are you okay?" Parker asks as he rests the phone against his shoulder so that he can fasten his shirt sleeve.

"Erm, yes, er, I think so. What are we doing tonight?" She asks, attempting to restore some kind of normality in her brain.

"We're eating in the restaurant here. I figured you'd be shattered so I've booked us a table. Are you ready?"

"Well, no, not really," she responds diving out of the bath. "I don't have anything to wear."

Parker laughs. "Sure you do. You packed at least one dress, didn't you?"

Now it was Laurels turn to laugh. "Mmm, I packed a few more than one, but they are no good to wear...here."

"Laurel." Parker says. "As long as you're in them and you're comfortable, they are good enough. You'd look good in a bin bag so pick one and hurry. I need to spend as much time with you as possible. Without a wall between us."

Laurel laughs, hangs up the phone and heads to the bedroom to unpack. *Strange. Where's my case?* She opens the walk-in wardrobe door to see all her clothes have been ironed and are hanging up. Her shoes are all neatly lined up on the wardrobe floor. And all her underwear is neatly stacked in the chest of drawers next to the wardrobe.

Who? How? What the...?

"Knock, knock, can I come in?" Parker calls as he gently pushes the dividing door open. "Are you decent?" he asks as he leans on the door to close it.

Laurel has her back to him. He stares at her reflection in the mirror. She's wearing the prettiest green and pink dress he's ever seen. Tiny pink butterflies dance along the dark green cotton of the knee length dress. The flat glitter covered sandals finish off the stunning outfit. A tiny gold butterfly necklace hangs just between her breasts. Parker stares a little too long as Laurel turns and catches him.

"What's wrong?" she asks as she clocks the look on his face. Her earlier elation threatening to drain away in the blink of an eye.

"Nothing's wrong, Laurel. You look beautiful."

She smiles as he walks over to her and pulls her into his embrace. "Here's me thinking I needed to buy you a wardrobe full of clothes and you wear this." He strokes the thin straps as he looks into her eyes. "You really are beautiful, Laurel." Resisting the temptation to take her mouth in his, he releases her and grabs her hand. "Come on, let's go eat. I'm ravenous." *And not just for food.* He muses.

Once they are seated at the table. Parker asks, "you sounded a bit strange on the phone earlier, is everything okay?"

Laurel is staring at the menu. One half of it seems to be in a foreign language, and the other, supposed English half, she couldn't make head nor tale of either. She looks up. Straight into his gorgeous brown eyes. Glad she's sitting down. Her legs wouldn't have held her up, had she been standing. Shaking the thoughts away, she'd almost forgotten about the phone call and the radio.

She blushes and tells him what happened. "I'm still not sure whether I dreamt it or not, to be honest."

Parker is grinning from ear to ear. "I wondered whether you would hear it."

"So, I didn't dream it then?" Laurel is gobsmacked.

"No, you definitely didn't."

"But... how... I'm confused." Laurel admits as she casts her eye back over the menu. "And I'm even more confused by this menu." She crosses her hands in her lap as she looks back up at him, waiting for him to laugh at her. He doesn't.

"Oh, Laurel. This life is all new to you, isn't it?"

"Yes. Until a few weeks ago I was a part time receptionist and a 2-bit club singer... if I was lucky. Now I'm staying in a 5-star hotel where the walk-in wardrobe is bigger than my flat and some random radio station has just played my song." Saying it out loud sounds like a child whining to her ears but Parker is watching her intently.

She takes her hands from her lap and places them on the table, fiddling with the serviette to distract her, not only from her...predicament... but from his eyes that want to bore into her soul.

Thursday 22nd December 2022

Laurel stretches her aching limbs out as the mist rises above the wild garden. She can see it from the floor to ceiling windows in her room. She was so tired last night she didn't even close the curtains. She's glad now though. The view is breath-taking. Bright evergreens with twinkling Christmas lights enhanced by the backdrop of rolling hills. She turns onto her side to get a better look. Everything about this mini break is... breathtaking. The hotel, the views, and... Parker. *I asked heaven for an angel, and it sent me you.* Laurel smiles dreamily as she remembers Parker walking her to the bedroom, kissing her cheek, and wishing her goodnight before he closed the interconnecting door.

Climbing out of bed, she heads to the bathroom to take a cool shower. As she touches the spot on her cheek where he'd kissed her, tingles of pleasure flow through her veins like bolts of lightning. Her breath catches as she switches the shower on as cold as she can stand it. Apparently, it's good for you… right now she begs to differ. Dithering, she turns it up and lets the warm jets pummel away the tiredness. She's looking forward to spending the day with Parker. He intrigues her.

Parker rises at the same time as Laurel and has an ice-cold shower himself, as he does every morning. It invigorates him for the day, not that he needs it today. He's looking forward to getting to know Laurel properly.

At 8:30 there is a knock on the main door of the suite on Laurel's side. She answers to an array of breakfast options, all the colours of the rainbow and enough food to feed a small army.

"Parker," Laurel knocks the interconnecting doors as the hotel waitress lays the food out on the coffee table in the centre of the room.

Parker answers looking even more devilishly handsome than he did the night before. The sight takes her breath away as she moves to allow him into the room.

"Are we expecting company?" she manages to ask once she's regained her composure.

"No. Why?"

"There's so much food here."

"Mmm, there is rather, isn't there. Would you prefer to invite Brian, or send some down to the soup kitchen?"

The waitress interrupts their conversation. "Excuse me, Sir, Miss, Mr Brian has already eaten. He says to tell you he's left the paperwork he needs signing with Clifford, and could you please sign it before you go out for the day?"

Parker looks up at her. He hadn't noticed she was there before; he was so captivated by Laurel.

"Ah, okay, thank you, Bethany."

"You're welcome, Sir."

Bethany leaves quietly as they sit down to enjoy breakfast.

"Soup kitchen it is then." Laurel says as she takes a mouthful of croissant, most of it landing on the plate it's so crumbly.

"Good choice." He grins.

"I would have said that anyway. I hate to see good food go to waste."

"A girl after my own heart." He responds as he catches her eye. His heart skips a beat as he watches her throat when she swallows the last of her green tea.

They are both dressed in jeans, t-shirts, and jumpers. They grab their winter coats as they set out to go ice skating. Parker writes a note for the food to be sent to the soup kitchen. Nobody knows how much he donates to them already, even though he's only normally here once a year. They saved his life once, and he'll never forget it.

"Ready?" he asks as he grabs her now gloved hand and guides her to the lift.

"As I'll ever be."

Parker feels the tension vibrate through her arm to his. "Are you nervous?" he asks, concern etched on his face.

"I am a little," She responds. "I didn't think I would be, but I have a weak spine and I don't want to fall. Maybe I shouldn't do it."

"Nonsense. You have strong legs, you'll be fine."

The lift delivers them to the hotel's reception, and they exit the doors straight into the waiting limo. *Wow, that's service for you.*

"Morning, Miss." Clifford says as he doffs his cap and closes the door behind her. Parker walks around and let's himself in the other side.

"Good morning, Clifford." Laurel answers as she settles into the armchair like seat.

On their 20-minute journey, Parker points out all the landmarks and famous places. He tells some of the horror stories of things that happened there centuries ago.

"Blimey, Parker. You are a mine of information; how come you know so much about this place?"

Parker realises his faux pas. He's never brought a girl with him when he's toured here, and he's torn between telling her the truth and telling bare faced lies.

"You were born here, weren't you?" she asks.

"Yes, yes, I was. Oh, we're here." *Saved by the bell*, relief washes over him.

Clifford let's Laurel out, and Parker takes her hand to lead her into the temporary building. After listening to the safety instructions and fitting the ice skates to their feet they head onto the rink. It's quiet this morning, most of the locals are doing their last-minute shopping, it won't get busy until the schools finish for the holidays at lunchtime.

"This is so...quaint, Parker. How long has it been here? It looks new."

"It's a temporary thing. They do it every year in this park. It's been going for about 10 years, I think. On and off, of course."

"It's so realistic. It feels like we're in the north pole." She says as she looks around her in awe. Singing reindeer, spray snow, and huge Christmas trees surround the skating rink.

"It's beautiful, isn't it. Come on, let's skate."

Laurel tentatively places her right foot on the ice and wobbles around.

"Don't think about it, Laurel, just go for it. The more you think, the more likely you are to fall." He grabs her hand and gently pulls her onto the ice.

"You've done this before then." She states as he releases her hand after a few minutes and performs fancy pirouettes.

"Yes, once or twice." He winks at her.

Laurel, steadier on her feet now, spins around. Keeping near to the fencing, just in case. She feels elated. She's never done this before but she's thoroughly enjoying herself. She feels alive. So much has happened in such a short space of time. "Life is awesome." She shouts out as she does one last spin before heading off the ice.

Parker catches up with her. "Did you enjoy that, Laurel?"

"I loved it, thank you so much. What time is it?"

Parker looks at his wrist. Yes, he still wears a watch. He's old school. "Blimey, it's almost 1pm."

"It can't be," She exclaims. "It feels like we've only just got here."

"Time flies when you're having fun, Laurel. Are you hungry yet?"

Even after all that breakfast Laurel feels a little peckish. *Must be all this exercise.* She thinks to herself.

"Mmm, I am a little. I quite fancy a hot chocolate and a portion of fries."

Unsure where that came from as she doesn't usually have either, she looks across at Parker tying the laces on his trainers. His profile is as stunning as his portrait. Her heart melts a little as he stands and pulls her into his arms.

"Hot chocolate and fries coming up, beautiful lady." She smiles up at him. His eyes pierce her soul. Again. She so wants to place her hands on his cheek and kiss him but she dare not. She simply cannot fall in love with this man.

Assuming they were going to a famous burger restaurant, Laurel is surprised when they walk a few paces to a food hut. It's only then that she realises this is all part of the Christmas markets these big towns and cities have taken to having. She's never been before, thinking it too commercialised, but she rather likes the feel of it.

"What are you having, Parker?" She asks as she places her order at the counter while he studies the menu on the chalkboard at the side of the servery.

"I rather think I'll have what you're having."

"Make that two, please," she says to the young woman taking her order and takes a £20 note out of the pocket of her jeans.

"What are you doing, Laurel?" He asks as he takes his card out of his pocket.

A little confused by the question as she would have thought it was obvious what she was doing, she turns to him. "I'm getting lunch." She's tempted to say *what does it look like I'm doing? Knitting.* But she refrains.

"I'll get it."

"It's done."

"Laurel. I didn't ask you here then expect you to pay."

Laurel is taken aback. "Whilst I can't afford to pay the hotel prices, I can buy us lunch."

"But you don't need to."

"So, it would seem, but I want to."

They say no more and stand aside to wait for their order.

Later that evening, after a little window shopping and a lot of talking, Laurel falls into bed and reminisces over the day's events. Her first proper romance seems about to blossom. Parker had listened intently to her throughout the day, he didn't give much away about himself, but she sensed he wasn't entirely happy. Drifting off into a dream filled sleep, Laurel slept like a baby.

Parker climbs into his bed, shocked at himself that he hasn't already made love to the beautiful creature sleeping in the adjoining room. *What the hell is wrong with me?* He ponders as his mind takes him through the wonderful day they've just had. He thinks back to lunchtime. Shocked at her insistence to pay, he respects her even more and is pleased that he's found someone who wants him. Not just his money.

"Yes. I do. And I'm very grateful. It feels good to finally get it off my chest."

"You still have work to do but you can let go of the guilt now. It was an accident, Parker. It's time to accept that and stop beating yourself up."

"Yes, I know, thank you, Laurel. Driving past the house has been strangely cathartic. I lived that day again talking to you, but maybe I can finally put it to rest."

"I hope so, Parker. I hope so."

"Now you know why I'm a comedian. I use comedy to hide my shame and guilt. I stand on stage and become someone else, instead of being me."

Laurel is stunned. "What's next for you then, Parker? Are you going to give up the comedy?"

"I don't know, Laurel. I always wanted to be in the background. Organising the events and promoting others."

"Oh, a bit like the work Brian does, then?" Laurel asks.

"Yes, exactly like that. Maybe we should do a job swap." Parker laughs, only half joking. "I've been working on ideas for that variety show I mentioned." Parker suddenly blurts out as he jumps from the sofa to fetch his laptop. The emotion of the past hour is seemingly forgotten.

Laurel is pleased. *This will really give him something to throw his passion into.*

Parker retakes his seat and shows Laurel his plans.

"Wait!" She exclaims as she reads the list of acts, he wants her to appear at the event. "Why on earth is my name listed as the headline act?" Her eyes open as wide as saucers as she stares at the screen.

"Because I've heard the album you've just cut with Petra and it's the best album I've heard in years. There is so much… heart and soul in it." He responds, staring into her eyes.

Laurel had almost forgotten the recording sessions she'd been doing with Petra; she had been so concerned about Parker.

"I put everything into those sessions," Laurel whispers. "My heart, soul and energy."

"I know. I can tell. Did you write all the songs yourself?" Parker asks.

"Yes. Why?"

"Some of them are so…raw."

Laurel looks at him. She feels like he's staring into her soul as well as her eyes when he looks at her, and she doesn't want his pity. She looks away.

"Look at me, Laurel," Parker says as he gently touches her chin and pulls her head up to face him. He wipes the stray tear away with his thumb. "Your turn now."

Laurel shakes her head. Most of her songs are about unrequited love and she's starting to feel foolish.

"No," She whispers. "I can't."

Parker knows not to push. He's been out with many women in his time, and he's learned a thing or two. He doesn't want to push her away. Glancing at his watch he notices it's almost lunchtime. "Come on, let's go and get something to eat." He takes her hands in his and pulls her to her feet. Hugging her gently before he releases her and leads her out of their suite and into town.

Christmas Eve - Saturday 24th December 2022

Laurel wakes to a gentle tap on the door. It's still dark outside although it's almost 8:30. Rousing herself, she climbs out of the luxurious king-sized bed, grabs the fluffy hotel robe from the chair, and pads over to the door. Glancing through the tiny hole in the middle of the door, she sees a man in a uniform. Her heart races as she struggles to open the door, fearing something has happened to Parker.

"Good morning, Miss. Mr Small has asked me to give you this." The man hands her a thick embossed cream envelope. In almost military-style precision, he doffs his hat, clicks his heels together, and walks away. Laurel stares after him. Her heart rate finally coming back to something close to normal as relief washes over her. Wrapping herself further into the robe, she climbs back under the covers and opens the envelope.

Dear Laurel,
You are cordially invited to Parker Small's end of season party to be held at the Blue Dolphin Hotel on 24th December 2022.

Wow, I didn't know there would be a party. This is wonderful. Laurel can barely contain her excitement.

Dress code: Ball gown/dinner suit.

Oh bugger! Laurel exclaims. *How the hell can I accept? The one thing I forgot to pack was a ball gown.*

93

She laughs to herself. The excitement she felt a moment ago drains from her body leaving her slumped on the pillows. *Where the hell am I going to get a ball gown from at such short notice?* Parker has put her in an awkward position. Still wrapped in her hotel robe she stomps over to the adjoining door and knocks, a little too loudly.

Parker, fully dressed and looking hot, opens the door. "Good morning, Laurel, did you get the invite?"

Totally thrown, Laurel takes a step back. "Erm, yes, er, thank you, I did, but…"

Parker stares down at her, searching her eyes. "But what, Laurel?" Panic rises in him. She looks… lost, scared and a little confused. "It's our traditional end of season party. We do it every year. Nothing to worry about." He says as he moves back into his room.

Laurel follows him, feeling flustered and embarrassed. "I can't come, Parker." She blurts out to his retreating back.

"Whyever not?" He asks as he spins around on his heel and stops abruptly. Laurel almost collides with him, but he catches her and holds her at arm's length, searching her face. "Laurel, what's wrong?"

Her eyes stare at the floor. She isn't upset. She's out of her depth. She is determined to always be honest with him, so she blurts out. "I don't have anything to wear." Even she realises how whiny it sounds and when Parker begins to laugh uncontrollably, she laughs too. "God that sounded so… bad… childish… cliché," Laurel says when they finally gather themselves together.

"Oh, Laurel. Your innocence floors me." Parker pulls her into him and whispers in her ear. "Go and get dressed. We have an appointment in an hour."

Unable to resist, Parker pats her bottom as she walks back to her room to shower and change. Laurel revels in the feeling. She feels so good in his arms. Wondering how an 'appointment' will help sort out her clothes dilemma, Laurel throws her dressing gown off, and walks into the shower, luxuriating under the gentle flow of the water.

An hour later she is standing in the most opulent boutique shop she has ever seen. The chandelier taking centre stage calls to mind the opening scene from '*Phantom of the Opera.*' Her favourite show. *Wow.* She mutters as she wanders around, staring. Not daring to touch any of the exquisitely designed dresses and gowns.

"Laurel, this is Mandy. She will fit you for your gown." Parker introduces a tall lady with an Adam's apple whose smile instantly puts Laurel at ease.

In Mandy's company, she feels safe. Like she belongs. Barely having time to take in everything that's happened in the last couple of days, her mind wonders as Mandy takes her measurements, grabs her hand, and leads her to the dressing rooms at the rear of the boutique. "Take a seat in there, gorgeous lady and I'll bring a couple of dresses in for you."

Laurel sits on the fluffy cream coloured 2-seater sofa. *Blimey. This room is bigger than my flat!* Laurel exclaims as Mandy leaves her to fetch the dresses. Laurel lets her mind wonder again. She's enjoying herself for what feels like the first time in her life. She feels like she's meant to be there. The thought surprises her as she's always put herself down. And let others do the same.

The gentle buzz of her mobile phone ringing in her bag forces her out of her reverie. Messages galore from Petra,

Brian and most recently, Parker. *Why is he sending messages? He's standing outside.* Laurel opens the messages one by one and stares at her phone. Her hands shaking.

'Straight in at number 2 in the UK streaming charts. New singing sensation Laurel stuns with her debut single, "Love is.' Is the message which flashes up in all the texts. An excerpt from the national newspapers from yesterday morning. *Why didn't I receive these before now?*

"Parker, Parker. Laurel dashes out of the dressing room. Parker, where are you?"

Parker is chatting to Markus, the boutique's owner, and Mandy's other half.

"What's wrong, Laurel?" He asks as he breaks off his conversation.

"Nothing. Everything. I don't know." She staggers into a faint. Parker's bear-like arms catch her and pull her into his chest.

"Laurel, are you okay?" Markus asks. He too is a gentle giant and he's worried. The colour has drained from Laurel's face.

Parker picks her up and carries her back to the sofa in the dressing room. Reviving her, he strokes the back of her hand. "Laurel." He gently whispers. "Are you okay?"

Laurel looks at him and hands him her phone. "I'm more than okay, but… look."

Parker takes her phone and scrolls through the messages she points out to him.

"Have you only just seen these, Laurel?"

"Yes. My phone beeped while I was waiting for Mandy, and all these came through."

"So, you didn't know you'd got a hit single then?"

"Well. No." She answers, still in shock. "I have a hit single." She says out loud. As the reality of the situation kicks in, she reaches over to hug Parker. "I have a hit single." She says again. Releasing him she jumps up and down.

Parker watches, amusement lights up his eyes. *It's so good to see her happy.* He thinks to himself. Seeing her happy has somehow made him happier too. He holds his arms out to her.

"Thank you so much, Parker." She whispers into his chest as she falls into his embrace. "Thank you so much."

"You're welcome." He whispers back.

Their faces touch and heat radiates from them both. Without thinking, their lips find each other's. Their hearts race.

Laurel feels like she's on fire. The gentle touch of his lips sends shivers down her spine. She closes her eyes to savour the moment. Tasting him. He tastes of raspberry jam and peppermint tea. She gently inhales the sweet smell of mandarin and sage body wash. She is lost in him. Opening her mouth wider their kiss deepens. She feels like she wants to climb inside him, the kiss is so breathtaking.

His tongue slowly probes her mouth as if asking for permission to enter. Laurel accepts his tongue and places her hand behind his head. Lost in the headiness of the moment her sex begins to quiver and she deepens the kiss even more. She feels a connection to Parker she's never felt with anyone before. It scares her but she loses herself in the kiss.

"Right then, Laurel. Oops." Mandy exclaims as she enters the dressing room with the most gorgeous midnight blue ball gown.

Parker makes a sharp exit from the room, leaving Laurel in a high state of sexual tension.

He leans against the side of the dressing room, fearing his legs may give way underneath him. *Oh, my!* He exclaims. *That was one heady kiss. I don't think I've ever been kissed like that before. I lost myself in her. I never do that.*

"Parker. Are you okay?" Markus asks as he finishes serving a customer and wanders over to him. "You've gone a bright shade of pink."

"Yeah, I'm good, thank you." Parker answers, regaining his composure. They chat like the old friends that they are, while Laurel tries on several ball gowns and dresses. Mandy has been given a list of items Parker wants to buy for her. It is Christmas after all. And they have an important party to attend this evening. Plus, he wants to spoil her. So many women he's been out with have only ever wanted his money, but Laurel is different. He's lost count of the number of times she's paid for things for them since she arrived. He likes an independent woman. *She's going to be a bigger name than me.* He knows, without a shadow of a doubt.

Within an hour, Laurel is kitted out with all the clothes she needs. And more. They leave the boutique, promising to visit again soon and head to the limo parked in the side street next to the shop.

Climbing in, Laurel relaxes into the plush seats. "Thank you so much for everything, Parker. I'll pay you back for the dresses once I get some money through from Petra."

"You will do no such thing, young lady. These are my treat."

Catching the look in Laurel's eyes. He's seen that look before. Shock, gratitude and…doubt. "Think of them as Christmas presents and congratulations gifts."

Laurel, still learning that she is allowed to receive as well as give, smiles up at him and leans in to continue the kiss which was rudely interrupted.

Christmas Eve - Saturday 24th December 2022 - Evening

Parker, showered and dressed in a dark grey tuxedo knocks on the dividing doors between his and Laurel's rooms. It is 6:30pm and time for them to make their way downstairs for pre-party drinks.

"Coming," Laurel calls, fastening the strap on the 3-inch heeled silver sandals Parker had brought for her earlier. A simple silver diamond encrusted heart-shaped necklace with matching earrings complement the midnight blue ball gown. Laurel stands up straight and stares at herself in the mirror. *Wow. I look great.* Laurel is modest, but the dress she is wearing shows off her slender figure, and she feels great. *I made it.* She squeals to herself. Unable to jump for joy due to the constraints of the dress, but her heart is full to bursting with love. For herself, for Parker, Petra, and Brian. Grabbing her tiny silver purse she opens the door for Parker.

"Oh, my word," Parker stares at the vision before him, "You look stunning, Laurel."

Laurel performs an exaggerated curtsey, "Why thank you, kind sir." She giggles as she watches Parker's eyes roam around her body.

He offers his arm to her, and she takes it. Leading her through her room and out into the lift, it takes all his self-control not to throw her onto the bed and absent himself from his own party.

As they enter the lift, Laurel takes a minute to repay Parker's favour of looking her up and down. His rugged good looks, olive skin, and athletic torso take her breath away. *Grey suits him.* She thinks to herself as a smile tugs at the corner of her mouth. *Grey suits him very much.*

"Have you responded to your messages from earlier yet, Laurel?" He asks as the lift glides down to the basement room, thirty floors below, which Brian has hired for the party.

Brought back abruptly from her daydream, she answers, "Oh, my, I'd completely forgotten about those. No. And I left my phone in the room. I'll do it tomorrow." She nonchalantly waves her hand at him.

He laughs. "Tomorrow is Christmas Day, my lovely. Don't you think you should answer them today?"

"Oh dear. I'm losing all track of time. Yes, I suppose you're right. I'd better go back for my phone. Shall I meet you in there?" She asks.

"No, I'll come with you. You can send the messages and leave your phone there."

Pressing the penthouse button on the lift as soon as it reaches the basement Parker asks. "How come you didn't see the messages until today?"

"I'm not sure. I wondered that myself earlier, but I can only think it must be the signal. I haven't connected to the wi-fi as I only check my messages occasionally, and I've been having too much fun to think about them. I put my mobile data thingy on before we went out this morning, so that must have pushed them through."

"Ah. Now I understand. Good for you. I'm a slave to my bloody phone." He answers just as his phone lets out an almighty shriek. They both laugh at the timing. "See what I mean?"

Parker takes his phone out of his pocket as they enter Laurel's side of the suite. "Hey, little Bro, we're on our way. Laurel is just answering a few messages and we'll be down."

Laurel sits at the desk and answers the important messages from Petra, Brian, and Kim, then switches her phone off and throws it into the safe. Listening to Parker's half of the conversation.

"Really?" Parker says. "I don't think so, she hasn't said. Hang on I'll ask her."

"Laurel, have you received an email today from Brian about a photo shoot for a fashion magazine?"

Laurel hadn't thought to check her emails. She assumed everyone had closed their doors for the Christmas break. "I don't know. Why?" She questions as she tilts her head to one side trying to earwig the other side of Parker's conversation.

"Brian says can you check please and let him know your response when you get downstairs."

A curious look paints itself across Laurel's face as she retrieves her phone from the safe again. Switching it back on she scrolls through a stack of spam emails.

"Ah, here it is. She opens it and gasps. "Oh, my goodness. Look at this, Parker." Her hand shakes as she holds out her phone for him to read the screen.

"Woo hoo. That's fantastic, Laurel. He says as he hands the phone back to her. I assume you're going to say yes?" He questions. Looking at her face he thinks to himself. *Now it's sunk in.* He smiles as he watches her try to gather her thoughts.

"Can I… think about it?" She asks.

"Yes. You have until the lift deposits us at the basement lift doors."

"Eh? How come?"

"Because, dear Laurel, my darling brother will be waiting there for your answer."

"Really? Is he keen for me to do it then?"

"More than keen I would say but…" Parker sits next to her on the bed. "It has to be right for you, Laurel. Your life has changed virtually overnight. This is the new you. You are going to receive a lot of media attention. Brian and Petra will filter most of the garbage out. The fact that he's sent you the details means he's keen. He's worked with them before and trusts them."

Laurel's eyes widen. *I was born for this. I've slogged my guts out for 30 years. Now it's my time to reap the rewards.*

"It does seem like a great opportunity, I must admit. My eyes nearly popped out of my head when I saw the payment details though. Has Brian got that right?"

Parker takes her face in his hands. Looking into her eyes he responds, "Yes, it's right. And that's after Brian has taken his cut. He wants to manage you, Laurel. And I want him to. You're new to this and there are a lot of charlatans out there. We both want to look out for you."

Laurel is strong-willed but knows she needs their help. "That would be great, thank you both so much, but I want to see all the offers which are made to me. Not just the ones you or Brian think are worth pursuing." Laurel stares back into his eyes. She's no pushover and she wants to make sure he knows it.

"I'm sure that will be fine. We will arrange to meet after Christmas to sort the details out but, in the meantime, Brian will handle things for you. If anyone wants to work with you, give them his details and get them to contact him. He will make sure they don't mess you around or rip you off."

Although Laurel has only recently met Parker and Brian, she feels safe with them. She knows they have her best interests at heart. She is determined to do her best to look after them too. Laurel switches her phone off and places it back in the safe. "Do you think you could go one night without your phone?" She turns to Parker and holds her hand out.

It doesn't take him long to decide as he switches his phone off and hands it to her. "The most important people in my life are in this hotel." He answers as he takes her hand and leads her back to the lift.

The Party

Laurel and Parker make their way through the crowds in the basement and finally reach their designated table. Parker hasn't let go of Laurel's hand, despite many of the men at the party trying to prize her away. Every eye in the room has followed them. Parker pulls a chair out for Laurel and opens a bottle of champagne from the centre of the table. He pours them both a glass. He sits next to her and clinks glasses with her.

"Congratulations, Laurel."

"Thank you."

As predicted, Brian had been waiting at the lift doors for Laurel's answer. He was currently making the final arrangements for a photo shoot on the 28th December.

Parker talks to other people at the table as the catering team delivers the first of many courses of delicious food to the guests.

Laurel sits in stunned silence taking in everything that's happened to her in the last couple of months. She doesn't need to pinch herself to know what's happening, she's been working hard to make it happen. *I'm ready.* She smiles to herself. *This is what I'm here for. I can change lives with my music and that's exactly what I plan to do.*

"Hey, Laurel, you look amazing." Laurel is awakened from her reverie and jumps up from the table, almost knocking her drink over.

"Petra," she squeals. "I didn't know you were coming."

"Neither did I, but Brian called me yesterday and insisted I come. So much has happened in the last few days, and I wanted to congratulate you in person."

"Oh, thank you so much, Petra. I couldn't have done it without you. Or Brian and Parker. I will be forever in your debt."

"Nonsense, girl. We need to think about recording your next album. But these parties are legendary so tonight, enjoy yourself."

Petra kisses Laurel on her cheek and disappears into a crowd of partygoers hovering near the stage.

"Good evening, everyone, please take your seats for the first course of this evening's meal." Brian calls over the microphone.

The room's atmosphere settles into a gentle buzz as the meals are being savoured. A four-piece band play soft jazz music in the background.

"Parker," Laurel says as they await the final course.

He looks at her and waits for her to continue.

"How come you have the end of season party, in the middle of your tour?"

Parker laughs, "Ah you noticed then."

"Well, yes." Laurel smiles, waiting for his reply.

Instead of answering her, he rises from his seat and heads for the stage.

What did I say? Laurel ponders.

Parker grabs a microphone from one of the stands at the front of the stage and asks the band to take a break.

"Good evening, everyone. Thank you all for coming to this mid tour party. As you all know I like to see people happy, and I like to help others when I can. I've done extremely well for myself, and I can spot talent a mile off. I wouldn't be here if it wasn't for my dear friend Petra and my brother Brian. Please everyone, raise a glass to these wonderful human beings."

Glasses chink and 'to Petra and Brian' choruses around the room. When the cheers have died down, Parker continues.

"I intended this to be a small, intimate gathering," The room erupts again as there are fifty people seated around immaculately dressed lilac and silver tables. Over the noise Parker continues, "As you can see, I got a bit carried away with the invites."

Laughter erupts. Laurel watches intently as Parker moves across the stage. *He's a natural. And oh, so flippin handsome to boot.*

Parker carries on, "I did have another reason for throwing this party. A few weeks ago, I met a young lady."

Whoops, cheers, and wolf whistles drown out Parker's voice. Used to audience heckling, he waits patiently for the din to subside.

"This young lady has talent. Bags of it and I wanted to help her. Over the last few weeks, she's been recording music, and her debut single has gone straight to number 2 in the charts. Please put your hands together for Laurel. Laurel, please come onto the stage."

The room erupts in cheers and chants of, "Laurel, Laurel, Laurel."

Laurel is overwhelmed. She can barely feel her legs as they carry her to the stage. She feels like she's floating on a cloud. *I wonder if this is what they mean by an out of body experience.* She thinks to herself as she stands next to Parker.

"Congratulations, Laurel. This evening is for you, and we'd love it if you would perform your single '*Love is*' for us."

More cheers and whistles of encouragement energise the room as Laurel takes the mic from Parker. A small fizz of electricity passes through them both as their hands touch across the mic.

Laurel pushes the lump in her throat away as she turns to face the audience. A tear rolls down her face. *I did it.* "Thank you so much, Parker, Brian, and Petra. You have made a young, well youngish lady very happy." The audience claps. "This is a dream come true for me and I will always be indebted to you all. I can't thank you enough."

Laurel turns to the band to discuss the music, but the bass guitarist waves the music score at her. Only then does it occur to her that Parker had planned this all along and in a short space of time. She begins to wonder just who the audience is. It can't be his team, although she does recognise some of them from watching his shows as he always brings his team on stage at the end. Pushing these thoughts to the back of her mind she turns to face the audience and the band plays the opening bars of her song. You could hear a pin drop in the room. No one moves. No one seems to breathe. Even the tick of the clock on the wall remains silent. Laurel sings her heart and soul out and her music touches everyone in the room in different ways.

Parker leans against the wall and stares. *Wow. She's even better live.* Parker is in awe. *She has the voice of an angel.*

Laurel brings her song to a close to a standing ovation and ear-splitting claps, cheers, and whistles. Parker takes the microphone off her and hugs her close to him.

"Laurel, everyone." He says as the guests continue their applause.

The catering staff bring out the final course of the meal and the room falls back into a gentle buzz. Laurel and Parker retake their seats.

"Does that answer your question, Miss Laurel?" Parker laughs as he sits next to her.

She puts her arm around his shoulder and hugs him into her breast. "Yes, it does, and thank you."

Laurel finds an array of business cards, handwritten notes and booking requests when she returns from a trip to the bathroom. Reading them, she smiles. Some of them she has no intentions of responding to, but some look promising. She shows them to Parker as they leave the party whilst it's in full swing. Neither of them has drunk a lot as they don't want sore heads on Christmas Day.

Laurel uses her thumbprint to open the door of their suite. She enters first, throwing her little bag onto the desk in the corner of the room. She leans against the back of the chair to take her sandals off then throws herself on the bed. Exhausted but the happiest she's ever been.

Rolling onto her back she is surprised to see Parker still standing at the door. He closes it and leans against it, watching her intently.

"Parker are you okay?" She asks as she sits up, preparing to take her dress off.

Shaking himself out of his reverie he looks down at her.

"Yes, yes, I'm fine. I was just thinking about work, that's all."

"Oh, Parker, it's Christmas. Don't think about work now."

Parker looks at his watch. "Merry Christmas, Laurel," he says as he moves towards her. "It's one minute past midnight." His voice is gruff as he grabs her hands and pulls her up off the bed into a bear hug.

Laurel melts at his touch. Resting her head on his shoulder she responds. "Merry Christmas, Parker."

Looking up she stares into his gorgeous brown eyes. Feeling heady from the champagne and the joy of singing to a room full of people who actually wanted to be there, she takes the lead and stands on her tiptoes. Her mouth finds his and she gently nibbles his bottom lip, pulling his face towards hers. She gives herself to the kiss, almost feeling like she's losing her mind. Every nerve ending in her body sings in anticipation as his hands wander slowly down her back, pulling down the zip of her dress as they go. The dress glides over her hips and puddles at her feet. Laurel barely notices as her tongue plays with his. In one deft move, he picks her up and places her gently on the bed. He stares at her body. It blows his mind.

"Laurel, you are beautiful." He whispers almost to himself. She stretches on the bed and tries to roll on her side. Parker places his hand gently on her shoulder, "Let me look at you, Laurel. You're gorgeous. I want to take you. Right now. But I have to make sure you're okay with this."

Laurel so desperately wants to blurt out I love you, but she's come unstuck in this situation before, so she holds her tongue. Feeling the moment has been lost she curls herself up in a ball.

"I don't want a one-night stand, Parker. I want a proper relationship but we're so busy I can't see how it could work."

Parker, still fully clothed, sits beside her on the bed and pulls her into him.

"I want you more than anything in the world, Laurel, I will make it work." Parker strokes her face as he stares into her eyes. She feels he is touching her soul; he's looking so deeply.

"I will too." She whispers as she relaxes into his embrace and traces her finger down his face, over his shoulder and strokes his nipple.

His breath catches as she slides her fingers between the buttons of his pale blue silk shirt and gently tugs at a chest hair. She unbuttons his shirt with such a tender caress that he feels lightheaded. No one has ever touched him this way before. Their connection is so pure on all levels. He lets her take his shirt off then he lies beside her, stroking her arm he pulls her bra strap over her shoulder and plants gentle kisses along her arm. Deftly unclipping her bra with one hand he pulls it off and gazes as her pert breasts stare up at him. Trying hard to keep his breathing steady, he bends down and runs his tongue over her nipples. Her back arches in delight as tingles flow through her body, and little purrs escape her lips. He feels himself growing harder the more she seems to enjoy herself.

Her hands caress his torso and work their way down to his trousers. She slowly unzips them and pulls them off, throwing them on the floor. He's commando and she can't help but stare at his manhood. She desperately wants him inside her, but she feels him tense up as she reaches for him.

"Parker," she whispers, "are you okay?"

He plants tiny kisses on her breasts and then looks up at her.

"Yes, are you?"

"Yes, of course. I felt you tense up. Are you sure you're okay?" she asks, concern etched on her face.

"I thought you tensed, that's why."

"Oh, did I? I'm not used to this, I guess, I'm a little nervous, maybe it's that?"

Parker lies on his side and pulls her towards him, still on her back. Unsure what makes him ask, he says, Laurel, are you a virgin?"

"No, I'm… scared. I've had so many failed relationships and I'm a survivor of sexual abuse… I get twitchy when I get close to men."

He's shocked. Knowing the chances of anything happening tonight are slim to none he reassures her, and then climbs under the covers. She follows. Relaxing into each other's arms, Parker says, "Tell me more." He wants to know everything about her.

Laurel doesn't even know where to begin and says so. "I've had relationships but whenever they've got passionate or sexual, I've always backed off. I've never wanted casual affairs and I've always had the feeling that's what they wanted. Despite them saying otherwise, and that's what's always happened. I don't want this to be one of those 'flings.' *No way am I telling you the other stuff.* Laurel stops to take a breath, not daring to look up at him for fear of what she might see in his eyes.

He takes a breath and despite desperately wanting to make love to her, he pulls her face to his and kisses her, long and gently. "Laurel. I know we haven't known each other long but I know this is meant to be. I've never waited for a woman before, but I want you to be ready. I want all of you. The good times and the bad."

Laurel does look up at him now, "I want the whole 9 yards, Parker. Love, support and the fairy-tale wedding."

114

"And you shall have it." Parker kneels up onto his haunches. "Laurel Sage Rivers. I love you and I want to spend the rest of my life with you. Will you marry me?"

Shocked, Laurel looks up. The sincerity in his eyes melts her heart and soul. "Yes, yes, I will." Breathless, she thinks. *Wow, that's the best Christmas present. Ever.*

She leans in and kisses him. Hard and desperate this time, her brain explodes with happiness. She knows this is right. Even though it's quick. She just knows. And so does he. Falling into a deep sleep, they both dream of the future.

Christmas Day - Sunday 25th December 2022

Laurel and Parker wake early on Christmas morning, excitement fills the air.

"Good morning, gorgeous." Parker whispers as they uncurl their limbs from each other, and Laurel climbs out of bed to use the bathroom.

"Good morning, handsome." She responds as she plants a kiss on his forehead. "What shall we do today?" Laurel laughs as she climbs back into bed, wanting to make the most of the closeness before she heads home tomorrow.

"Well. It is Christmas Day, and as things have taken an… unexpected turn. I rather think we should stay in bed and… get to know each other." Parker responds, stroking Laurel's arm. When he glances up and sees the look in her eyes, he knows he's made a mistake. *How stupid can one man get?* Parker wishes the ground would swallow him whole. *She told you yesterday she was scared, and you let your mouth run away with you.*

Laurel bites her bottom lip; tears form in the corners of her eyes. *How do I tell him I want him so badly, but I also want to wait?*

Trying to make amends for his mistake, he throws the covers off them and pulls her off the bed, "Come on, let's get showered and dressed. We have some celebrating to do."

Why can't I just go with it and enjoy the moment. Sex or no sex. Laurel curses as she takes a long cool shower. Every inch of her body longs for Parker's touch.

Parker takes a cool shower in his adjoining room. *Why do I always let my dick do the talking.* He yells to himself as the water needles every pore of his being. He has an erection just thinking about her and turns the temperature down even further to try and get rid of it. *What are you doing to me, Laurel?* Knowing he must tread carefully, he doesn't want to lose her, he walks out of the shower and dresses in his most comfortable jogging bottoms and hoodie before going back through to Laurel's half of their suite.

He stops in his tracks as he watches her dry her hair. The loving energy he feels radiating from her body is enough to draw him to her. He stands behind her and rests his hands on her shoulders while she puts her hair up into a ponytail.

She is wearing a long plain blue dress; the colour matches her eyes. Parker takes her hand, and they leave the suite.

"Where are we going?" She asks as they climb into the limo. "And do you ever give your staff the day off?" Clifford closes the door behind her, and she settles into her seat.

"We are going for Christmas Day breakfast at Brian's and yes, I do, but Clifford insisted on driving us. I hope you have plenty of room for food. Brian's partner is the best chef in Scotland."

Laurel claps her hands, "Ooh, goodie, I'm starving."

Breakfast is the most wonderful experience Laurel has ever had. Brian's partner, Stef, really is the best.

Parker tells them about the engagement and the champagne flows. When they finally leave after lunch, (Stef insisted,) they are both very tipsy and very full.

"Oh, my word, Parker. That was wonderful. I think I may sleep for a week after all that food."

He laughs. "I know. I try to fast for a week before I go to Brian's, Stef has always been like that."

"Ah, he's lovely, Parker. Are they married?"

"No. They've been together so long now I don't think it's entered their heads to get married."

"They seem so happy. I'm pleased. Brian is such a lovely man."

Parker nods. "Yeah, he's pretty cool for a brother and a manager."

Once Clifford has dropped them off at the hotel, he leaves and takes the rest of the day off.

Laurel and Parker head to the suite and as they open the door Laurel gasps in amazement.

"Parker, what's all this?" She asks as she stares at the array of presents on the bed.

"Merry Christmas, Laurel." He grins as he sits down and starts to hand the presents to her.

"Are all these for me?"

"Of course, you deserve to be spoiled. Come on. Open this one."

Jewellery, experience days, clothes and goodness knows what else are strewn around the room as Laurel opens the presents.

"Parker, this is too much." Laurel sees the look in his eyes and realises he's getting as much out of giving her these presents as she is out of receiving them.

She's never been spoiled like this before and feels quite emotional. "These gifts are perfect. How did you know… and why have you spent so much? I haven't got you anything."

"You have, Laurel, you've given me everything I could ever wish for. Your hand in marriage."

"But…"

"No buts, Laurel. This is your life now. What's mine is yours. Laurel is overwhelmed by his generosity.

"Thank you, Parker." She throws her arms around him and hugs him close.

"You're welcome, Laurel. Oh, and I spoke to your friend Kim. She told me what to get."

"Kim, how do you know Kim?"

"My security team traced her, and my secretary called her on Friday."

Laurel is astounded. "Should they have done that? Isn't that…wrong?"

Parker shrugs. "Probably. But I didn't want to go through your phone to get her details and I remembered her from the competition."

Laurel raises an eyebrow. "Did you now?"

"Well, she's not exactly hard to miss, is she? And she was very in my face at the backstage gathering."

Laurel smirks. "Yep, that's Kim."

Boxing Day Monday 26th December 2022

Parker heads back into the hotel after closing Laurel's door on the limo. Tears bubble in the corner of his eyes as he turns back to wave. Too late as Clifford has already sped off into the Boxing Day traffic.

Feeling like he's lost his right arm, no woman has ever had this effect on him before, Parker ambles back to the suite. Opening the door to the heady scent of her lavender and jasmine perfume, he sinks onto her bed. Replaying the last few days over and over in his memory. Storing them for later times when he's feeling low.

Shaking himself out of his reverie he heads to his own room to pack his belongings. His final show in Scotland is this evening and the tour travels south in the early hours.

Laurel's head is full of thoughts of the last few days and of the future. She lets herself daydream of stage lights, tour buses and cheering crowds. The buzz of the intercom pulls her back from her glorious daydream.

"Miss Laurel," Clifford calls.

Laurel presses the intercom next to her and calls back, "Yes, Clifford."

"There seems to be a problem, Miss."

Laurel's heart sinks. "What's the problem, Clifford?"

"It appears, the train company is on strike. All trains have been cancelled."

Laurel opens the window and stares at the front of the station. A mixture of handwritten and digital signs stare back at her, daring her to react. They all read the same. 'Due to industrial action, there are no trains running today,

121

26th December. Please find alternative transport. Further disruptions may occur over the new year period.'

Bloody marvellous. Laurel curses under her breath as she climbs out of the limo and heads towards the customer service desk in the middle of the concourse. Intending to seek 'alternative arrangements' which she assumes will be a bus. Well, several buses to be precise. *I assume this strike is over pay. Do they not think of the inconvenience to others? And what happened to people doing a job because they love it?* Laurel huffs as she stomps closer to the desk.

 Clifford watches her sashay towards the crowd as he too climbs out of the car. He follows close behind and is almost crushed in the stampede.

"Laurel, Laurel, Laurel. We love you, Laurel. Sing us a song." Wolf whistles, cat calls, and screams render Laurel speechless and motionless as a crowd descends upon her, pulling at her clothes. Within seconds a camera flashes and a microphone is thrust under her nose.

"Laurel, Laurel, how does it feel to be an overnight sensation?"

Laurel can't move. No matter how hard she tries. Her legs won't do as she tells them, and even if they did, she hasn't anywhere to go. You couldn't get a piece of paper between her and the crowd.

"Miss Laurel. Miss Laurel," Clifford calls as he picks up speed and follows her perfume, pushing his way through the crowd. "Miss Laurel, are you okay?" He asks when he finally reaches her.

All Laurel can do is nod as Clifford takes her by the arm and all but carries her to safety.

Wednesday 28th December 2022

Laurel somehow manages to avoid the journalists as she heads for the supermarket to do her weekly shop. She is greeted with many a funny look, a fair few handshakes, and more hugs than she's had in a lifetime. And that was just getting out of the car! *Wow.* She mumbles to herself as she grabs the carrier bags from the boot and puts her coat on so she can put her hood up. Her glasses are reactalight and she prays that will be enough to discourage further well-wishers. Not. A. Chance. Knowing nothing will stop them crowding her she politely asks them all to back off so that she can shop. Amazingly, they do. *Must be because I asked nicely.* She muses. Phone camera flashes almost blind her as she wanders up and down the aisles. Thankfully, because it's so early, there aren't too many people about, so she makes the most of her shop. She knows it will be the last one she will do herself for quite a while. Being a positive person, she smiles and engages with everyone as she always has done. She leaves the shop feeling a sense of overwhelm, but also relief. *This is my life now. I have to get used to it.* The ringing of her phone breaks her reverie.

"Hey, Petra. How are you, how was Christmas?" Laurel gushes as she presses the green button to answer.

"Hey, gorgeous overnight sensation," Petra responds, "I'm fabulous. Christmas was fabulous. Even better for you though, eh." Petra teases her.

"What do you mean?" Laurel is confused.

"Come on, Laurel, it isn't every day you go straight to number 2 in the charts, become an overnight sensation and…. this is the biggie… You become engaged to the country's most eligible millionaire bachelor."

"Woooahhhh. Whaaaattttt!" Laurel exclaims.

"Oh, and that is positively the last shopping trip you go on by yourself too."

Laurel shakes her head. "Woah, Petra, what the hell. I can't take it all in. What did you say about Parker, and how the hell did you know I'm at the supermarket?"

Petra laughs, "You are all over social media. Your fans are tagging you."

"What, where?"

"Everywhere you are, honey."

Laurel flicks through her social media accounts on her phone. "Jesus Christ." She exclaims. "These photos were only taken moments ago. How the hell…" Laurel laughs hysterically. *Well. I asked for fame and fortune. And it appears the universe didn't let me down.*

"Laurel. Are you okay?" Petra asks through the ear-piercing laughter.

"Yes, I'm fine, thank you. It's all just a bit… much." She answers.

"I know honey, that's why I'm calling. It's going to get even crazier now."

"Why, what's wrong, Petra?"

"Oh, absolutely nothing, darling girl. Everything is wonderful." Laurel waits as Petra talks to someone in the background.

"Laurel, you still there?"

Laurel is dazed. She is going over the entire conversation again in her mind. *Did I hear her right? The country's most eligible millionaire bachelor. No way!*

"Laurel. Laurel. Are you there?"

Forcing her out of her reverie, she answers. "Yes, Petra, I'm still here. Just a little dazed, to be honest."

"Well, prepare to be dazed and dazzled. Brian has been on the phone this morning as he wants to use the studio to do your photo shoot."

"Oh, okay, that sounds cool."

"It's better than cool, Laurel. The photo shoot is a pre-shoot for your UK tour. Which, by the way, begins on the 3rd January.

"My wha…aaaaa…tttt…" Laurel is dumbfounded. "What… how…er… help." Laurel squeals.

Petra, used to this from working with so many up-and-coming stars lets Laurel squeal and squeak.

"I'm sorry, Petra, I sound like a spoiled brat, don't I?"

"Not at all, honey. This is normal. It's all new to you but it's the life you should be living. You should see some of the comments. You are changing people's lives through your music."

"But…" Laurel stammers.

"No buts, Laurel. This is the life you were born for. I'll send you all the info now regarding the photo shoot this evening. Go home. Call Parker and chill. You're going to be one busy little bee from now on."

Laurel is relieved she has another day's grace. Petra's artist, who had stepped in when Laurel got stranded, has to record again this morning so she takes Petra's advice. Taking a few deep breaths to calm her nerves she drives slowly home, trying to take in everything that's happened in the last couple of weeks. Excitement and a little trepidation course through her veins.

I did it! She shrieks to herself as she pulls up outside her flat. She staggers through the door with her shopping just as her laptop wakes up with a video call notification.

Dropping the bags, she just catches the call and opens it to see Parker staring at her through the camera lens.

"How's my pretty, gorgeous, overnight sensation doing today?" He asks as Laurel flops on the sofa, laptop perched on the battered glass-topped coffee table.

Laurel's smile melts his heart. "She's good, thank you. A bit… discombobulated but good."

Parker grins at her. "I'm not surprised. I just spoke to Petra. I'm so excited for you, babe. Welcome to the wonderful world of showbiz."

Laurel relaxes as she and Parker talk about everything and nothing. She is shocked when he says, "We have a wedding to plan."

"Oh, my. I'd almost forgotten about that." She jokes. "How on earth are we going to fit that in? We are both going to be touring for the next 3 months."

"I know," Parker sighs, "and I miss you already."

"I miss you too."

Laurel takes the laptop into the kitchen along with the shopping bags so they can continue their conversation. She cooks a meal, while Parker orders room service and they eat together via video call.

"I wish I was there with you, Laurel. That looks delicious. Another of your many talents, eh, cordon bleu chef."

"Ha, I hardly think Spaghetti Bolognese would be classed as cordon bleu, but I must admit. It is delicious. I'm spoiling myself as it's my favourite meal."

"Good for you. You deserve it."

A silence descends as Laurel finishes her last mouthful. "What's wrong Parker, you look a little forlorn."

"Oh, I was just thinking, how are we going to keep in touch with such punishing schedules?"

"We'll be fine, Parker." Laurel is confident that everything will be okay. Parker isn't so sure. Already contemplating giving up his comedy gigs, being away from Laurel is going to be a real test for him.

Tuesday 3rd January 2023

Laurel is both buzzing with excitement and shaking with nerves. This is the first evening of her first tour. To start her off gently, Petra and Brian have ensured that she plays to small audiences to begin with. Although Laurel doesn't consider 5000 to be a small audience. The show is being recorded. Mainly so that Parker can watch it later, but also so that Laurel can watch it back and make any changes to her performance. The set seems a little over the top to Laurel but she is being guided by Brian. And Brian knows his stuff.

"This just isn't me, Brian," Laurel mutters as they stand in the wings waiting for the warmup act to finish.

"What isn't you, Laurel?"

Laurel flays her arms around and points to the rig. Dazzling fairy lights surround the stage. Hidden behind a curtain just in front of the band, her name in 6ft tall monochrome lights. The band. Her band. Waiting patiently for the stage to clear and the curtain to fall. *Her band.*

"Of course it's you. You've worked hard for this for years, Laurel. Enjoy it." Brian hugs her, and then holds her at arm's length. "You look stunning, Laurel. It's a shame I'm not straight. Parker wouldn't stand a chance."

Laurel laughs but she has to admit she feels good in the short, ruffled, silver one-strap sequined dress. Her red hair, recently curled, cascades across her right shoulder. She looks like a Greek goddess. And feels like one too. Born for the stage she removes the slippers she's been wearing all day and slides her feet into brand new designer black kitten heeled sandals. Feeling instantly grounded as she fastens the straps around her ankles, she's ready to take on the world.

"Go get 'em, Laurel," Brian shouts over the enthused cries of the waiting audience as he leans against the narrow wall to watch the show.

Laurel strides confidently onto the stage. She sits on the tall stool strategically placed in the letter U of her brightly lit name. This tour is made up of songs from her debut album, and being old school and traditional she sings them in order. Laurel grabs the microphone. She stares at the front row of the audience (the only row she can see with the bright stage lights dancing across her eyes.) Taking a deep breath, and without hesitation, she begins.

The first song is the hardest one to sing. The audience is in a frenzy. She can't see them, but boy can she hear them. *Wow. They are cheering for me.* Somewhat glad she can't see them, in case it freaks her out, Laurel sings her heart out. She's singing for herself, but also for them. The band are amazing, and she has never felt more alive. She pours her heart and soul into the performance and hopes that the audience didn't notice the couple of bum notes at the beginning.

An hour and a half later after whipping the audience into even more of a frenzy, she is shattered. She has danced, run, walked, and strutted around the stage. Very grateful she didn't wear stilettoes; she takes her place back on the stool to sing the final song of the show. The song that got her here, '*Love Is*.' The energy in the theatre is electric, and Laurel waits a few minutes for the audience to quieten down. She begins the song acapella style. The audience is silent. You could have heard a pin drop. If you strained your ears though, you would hear Brian crying.

"Touches your soul, doesn't it?" The stagehand whispers in Brian's ear as the band joins in for the final chorus.

Laurel leaves the stage to screams, shouts and chants of more, more, more. She falls into Brian's arms and sobs. "Oh, my God, Brian, that was amazing."

"Laurel, I'm speechless. Come on, you need to go back on and do an encore."

The band are leaving the stage too and a group hug ensues.

"Come on, Laurel," Brian coaxes her as the band make their way back onto the stage.

Laurel had insisted there be no encore, but she hadn't expected this reaction from the audience.

"Okay," she relents, "We'll do the last verse and the chorus of '*Love Is*.'"

Laurel walks back onto the stage to cheers. The auditorium lights are up, and the stage lights are dimmed. She gasps as she faces the sell-out arena. *Oh, my word. I did it.* Laurel stands centre stage, microphone in her hand and a lump in her throat. When the audience have finished cheering, she looks around.

"Thank you." She says into the microphone. "Thank you all for coming out tonight. I know the weather is horrible out there, but this is Great Britain." The audience laughter peels. "Thank you from the bottom of my heart. I hope you all enjoyed the show as much as I did. And I know this is always said, but you have been an amazing audience. This is the first show of my first tour, and it will always hold a special place in my heart. I couldn't have done it without you all." The audience are in uproar again. "Thank you also to the band." Laurel steps to the side of the stage and introduces each of the band members in turn.

"Thank you also to Petra my producer, and Brian my manager. I love you all." She screams as she turns to the band to give the signal to play.

Encore finished, Laurel bows and thanks the audience again before retiring to her dressing room.

Everyone piles into the tiny, freezing cold room to congratulate Laurel. Once they have all left, she and Brian sit and talk through the show.

"Brian, I can't thank you enough. I'm so overwhelmed with emotions, and I miss Parker so much." A tear escapes Laurel's eye as she leans her head on Brian's shoulder.

Brian rubs her back. "I know, Laurel, he misses you too."

"I'll call him when I get home tonight."

"He'll love that. Make sure you get plenty of sleep; we are leaving early tomorrow morning for the rest of the tour."

Laurel nods as she begins to collect her things.

"I'll leave you to it, Laurel. Congratulations."

Laden down with bunches of flowers, boxes of chocolates, and bottles of wine. Laurel takes a taxi back to her flat. When she comes back from her tour, she plans to look for something bigger.

As the venue is close to Laurel's flat, she is amazed to note that it has only just gone 11:30pm when she arrives home. The laptop, open on the kitchen table, is giving off the familiar buzz of an incoming video call. Laurel places everything on the kitchen worktop and dashes to answer the ring.

"Parker, hi," she squeals as his face comes into focus through the small screen.

"Laurel. You look amazing. How did it go? Brian sent me a couple of clips. You were fabulous." Parker gushes as Laurel sits down at the kitchen table, grabbing a bottle of water from the fridge on her way.

Laurel unexpectedly bursts into tears. "S…s…sorry, Parker." She stutters through the tears.

"Ah, Laurel, what's wrong?"

"N…noth…nothing… It's all good. In fact, it's great. I… I'm just… so happy... and overwhelmed."

Parker nods. He remembers his first time on stage in front of an audience and his reaction afterwards was much the same.

"Oh, Parker it was fantastic. I've never felt so happy, but I miss you so much." Laurel blurts out once her sobbing has subsided.

Parker stares at the camera, desperate to be with his fiancé but his punishing schedule means he's going to be away for the entirety of Laurel's tour.

"I miss you so much too, Laurel. This is your time to shine though. Concentrate on your singing and your tour."

"I know, Parker. I will." She sniffles but it doesn't stop the tug at her heartstrings.

"Time will fly, Laurel."

Laurel nods. Still reeling from the evening. "I'd better go, Parker. I still have to pack, and Brian is picking me up at 5am."

"Okay, gorgeous. Sleep well."

"You too." She utters as she disconnects the call. She could have sworn she heard him say, 'I love you,' as she pressed the end call button.

Drinking her bottle of water as she packs, Laurel is loving life. Finishing her packing in record time, she phones for a takeaway pizza then falls into bed and has the best, albeit shortest, night's sleep she's ever had.

Saturday 11th March 2023

The next three months fly by for both Laurel and Parker. Snatched conversations and sporadic messages become the norm, much to their chagrin.

Laurel has been home for a few days. She's had time to digest everything; the tour, her life, and her relationship, and she finds she is having cold feet. Not in the literal sense as it's quite warm for the time of year. This is what she's always wanted. To entertain others. And she loves it. She can't imagine life without it now. In a couple of weeks, she will be back in the studio to record her second album, and next week she has a meeting with Brian to discuss her next tour. The last meeting with Brian hadn't gone well as Parker was also there, via video link, trying to tell them what to do. Her relationship with Parker is strained. The few calls they have had in the last three months have left her feeling as if she is single again.

Having taken to drinking water instead of wine in recent weeks, due in no small part to a raging hangover and the worst performance of her career to date, she grabs a glass of water and pops a slice of lemon in and sits at her kitchen table with her laptop open. She stares at the screen willing it to give her the answer. She knows she shouldn't call Parker now. Her come down from the tour has hit her hard and she is having an off day, but she can't put it off any longer. She knows he's free tonight. It's his last night off before his tour ends next month. She dials his number from the app on her computer and waits. And waits. *That's odd.* He said to call tonight so they could discuss the call they'd had with Brian. Hanging up she makes herself a cheese and pickle sandwich and picks up her pencil and paper. An idea for a new song has just come to

139

her and she doesn't want to lose it. Twenty minutes later she's finished, and she sends a photograph of it to Petra. Another one to add to the list for the studio days.

She calls Parker again. As the call connects the screen stays black.

"Hi, Parker. How are you?" She asks. "Can you hear me?"

Strange noises in the background heighten her senses. *Is that a woman I can hear?* Laurel wonders.

"Hi, Laurel, yes, I can hear you. How are you?"

"I'm fine, Parker, why isn't your camera working?"

"Oh, I'm not sure. Hang on."

"Are you out and about?" Laurel asks as the screen flickers into life, and she sees Parker in amongst a large crowd.

"Yes, I'm out for a meal with some of the crew."

"Okay. I won't keep you then. Bye."

"Wait. No, Laurel, hang on. Let me find a quieter area in the restaurant. Upstairs is closed, I'll sit on the steps. Hang on."

Laurel stares at the screen waiting for Parker to settle. In her head, she has it all planned out. What to say, how to say it. How nice she would be. That all changes when she spots red lipstick at the side of his mouth.

As calmly as she can with her insides in knots, she looks straight at the screen, "It's over, Parker."

Parker hasn't even caught his breath from his climb up the stairs as he glares back at the camera.

"What. Why? What do you mean, it's over?"

"Exactly what I said. It isn't working." Feeling guilty because he has helped her so much and his brother is amazing, she asks, "Who wears red lipstick on the crew, Parker?"

Laurel met all the crew when she was there at Christmas. She knows none of them wore the garish shade of red on Parker's lips. "Or have you taken to wearing make up?"

Parker sighs. A deep, heavy, heart-wrenching sigh. "I'm sorry, Laurel."

"So am I, Parker, so am I." She answers. "Thanks for the memories but it's over. I'll leave the ring with Brian when I see him. Enjoy the rest of your tour." And at that, she ends the call. *Wow, that was easier than I expected. I knew something was wrong, but I never thought it would be another woman.*

Laurel feels surprisingly calm, which is unusual. She's been here before, too many times, but this time, she will move on. She has plenty to occupy her time. First things first she calls Brian to tell him the news, then she starts searching for her perfect home. She knows exactly where she wants it to be.

Saturday 1st April 2023

Recording of the new album goes smoothly. *I must be on the right path;* she ponders as she listens back to the final cut. *This all feels so… right. So easy and hassle-free. Is it too good to be true?*

"Is that a wrap?" Petra asks as she presses the button on the console next to her to speak to Laurel in the recording booth.

Grinning from ear-to-ear Laurel looks up at her through the small round window. "It's a wrap." Taking the earphones off she bounces out of the booth and hugs Petra. "Thank you so much, Petra. That was amazing."

"It was. I can't believe it's only taken us two days. I'd planned in right up to Easter, and including, if we needed it."

Once they finalise the release dates and tie up any loose ends, Laurel heads out of the studio and back to her flat. She hasn't been able to find her dream home, even though she's been looking every waking hour for the past few weeks.

Laurel now has a security officer watching her wherever she goes. He is so unobtrusive she often wonders whether he's actually there. He is. He is walking ten paces behind her, as he always does, so that the press won't hound her. She has no idea how she's avoided them for so long, but they have left her alone. *No doubt that will be different when the new album is released.* Laurel has never been happier, and she whistles to herself as she climbs the stairs to her flat. Rash follows close by.

Laurel stops in the alcove to her flat, her heart beating out of her chest. She leans against the wall waiting for Rash to catch up with her.

Seeing her hovering in the doorway, Rash races up the stairs two at a time, "Miss, are you okay?" He asks as he stands by her side.

Laurel nods at the door. Slightly ajar. She's positive she locked it when she left this morning.

Rash is 5' 9" tall and pure Indian muscle. Nothing fazes him. Except, of course, spiders. Rash doesn't do spiders.

Moving Laurel gently out of the alcove, he silently pushes the door open another inch. "Hello, who's there?" He calls as he steps quietly into the tiny porch. Given his size, he is stealthy. "Hello." He calls again as he slowly pushes down the handle of the solid wooden door which leads into Laurel's lounge.

"Hello. Who's there." He calls again.

"Surprise," Parker shouts as he thrusts a huge bunch of red roses in Rash's face. As quick as lightning, Rash grabs hold of Parker and pushes him against the wall.

"Miss Laurel. You can come in now." He shouts as he moves Parker away from the wall ready to escort him from the flat.

Laurel follows Rash's voice and stares, horrified at the sight before her. "Parker!" She exclaims. "What the hell are you doing breaking into my flat?"

"You know this guy?" Rash asks.

"Yes, indeed I do."

"Shall I let him go, Miss?"

Tempted to say, no, throw him out, Laurel is curious as to why he's here.

"Yes, please, Rash. You can let him go."

144

"Right you are, Miss. You know where I'll be if you need me."

"I do, thank you, Rash."

Laurel picks the flowers up off the floor where they landed when Rash had grabbed Parker, and places them on the kitchen table. "Care to explain yourself?" She asks as she fills the kettle and switches it on. More for something to do than the necessity of making a drink.

"Laurel, I miss you," Parker states as he takes hold of her hands and attempts to pull her towards him.

"Sorry, Parker." Laurel is steadfast and doesn't move an inch. "I'm not interested, and I'd really like you to leave."

Parker takes an envelope out of his pocket and places it on the kitchen table in front of him. Sliding it over to her, "Please read this, Laurel." He pleads.

She places her fingers gently on the corner of the envelope and pulls it towards her. Parker's fingers glance across hers and the effect on Laurel's heart is electric. *No.* She shouts to her fast-beating heart. *Do not lose your resolve. Read the letter when he's gone.*

Parker feels the electricity too and moves his hand away quickly, not wishing to upset Laurel any more than he already has.

"I'll read it when I get the chance." Laurel states as she places the envelope, alongside the rest of her post, behind the salt and pepper shakers on the kitchen worktop. "And before I forget, you'd better take this." Laurel removes the diamond encrusted engagement ring from the bottom of the fruit bowl where she'd thrown it after 'the call' that changed her life, again. She hadn't seen Brian to give it him and it wasn't fair to drag Parker's brother into their mess. Holding it out to Parker he stares into her eyes.

145

Don't look at me like that. She averts her gaze from his, turns around, and takes a mug out of the cupboard above her head. The picture of red squirrels balancing on slender snow-covered tree branches always makes her smile. She places a supermarket own brand green tea bag into the mug and re-boils the kettle. Still with her back to Parker she says, "Please leave." Burying the tears, she stares at the cupboard.

"I'm sorry, Laurel. Please read the letter." Parker begs as he closes the kitchen door behind him. Cursing himself under his breath. *I really hope she reads the letter. I don't want to lose her.* A voice inside his head screams, *you should have thought about that before.* Shaking his head at his stupidity, he leaves Laurel's flat and heads to the hotel two streets away. He's checked in indefinitely as he's determined to win her back.

Laurel allows the tears to roll down her face. The emotions of the last few weeks pour out of her. Her life has changed so much, and she just needs to switch off and let the world pass her by for a few hours. Taking her tea into the living room, she grabs a book off the top of a huge pile of 'to be read's' and settles herself on the sofa. *Trust me to pick a bloody romance.* She laughs despite herself as she becomes engrossed in the story. Not dissimilar to her own situation. *Funny that,* she muses, almost tempted to put the book down. Dreading a happy ending as she doesn't see one for herself and Parker, at this moment in time.

Her flat is small. As she's left the kitchen door open; she can see the letter Parker left sticking out from behind the condiments set. It's taunting her to read it. She's left things to fester before, so she takes the bull by the horns, throws the book on the sofa, and grabs the letter. Sitting at

146

the kitchen table, she stares at the envelope for a few minutes. The handwriting is exquisite, neat, tidy. Not at all like Parker's writing. Although she's seen it many times before, this time it feels… different. It feels like he's taken his time over writing to her. Even down to addressing the envelope. *He must have planned to post it.* She assumes as he's included her full address.

Taking a sharp knife out of the drawer to her left, she slices the envelope open and removes the letter. A photograph also falls from the envelope and lands face down on the table. The letter is written on hotel headed paper. The hotel he was staying in when they had 'that call.' Laurel takes a deep breath and begins to read:

My darling, Laurel,

I am writing this to try to explain how I feel about you. I've never been good with affairs of the heart and I'm not much better at writing, but here goes. I read all of the entries for the competition, the one you won last year, to see me perform some new material. They were all good. Some very good. Some excellent and I have passed some of them on to contacts of mine in the industry, hoping they will be published. Anyway, I digress. I told you I'm not good at this stuff. Your entry was the only one that was sent to us handwritten, and by post. That was the winning touch. The fact that you took the time to handwrite rather than type and to post it, I think I fell in love with you then. It got better though. When I read your entry, it took me back to my younger days and my mom telling me a story about my grandparents and how they met. The story was tinged with sadness, happiness, and giggles, and those were the emotions your story stirred in me. It was almost like my grandmother was speaking to me. Maybe she was, who knows? I felt such a strong connection to you and yours was the only story that gave me any such reaction. I passed the best three entries on to my team of judges which were a few of my touring crew. Most of them picked your story. Even if you hadn't won, I would have contacted you. We were destined to meet. Anyway, I'm rambling now so I'll get to the point.

Laurel pauses her reading to make herself another cup of green tea. The last one had gone cold, and she needs the warming sensation of the tea to help her read the rest of Parker's letter. Settling herself at the kitchen table again, she continues to read.

The day of our last call was the anniversary of my brother's passing. As you know, I rarely drink to excess, preferring to be in control, rather than controlled by anything or anyone. But for some reason, my emotions got the better of me that day and I'd had more than one too many. I missed you. I wanted to talk to you and share how I was feeling. Shed the guilt I've been carrying, but you weren't there. And no, I'm not trying to blame you, I'm trying to explain to you. Carrie, my PA, came into my suite to discuss the arrangements for the remainder of the tour as some of the schedule is quite tight. I'm not sure whether you've met Carrie but she's...

Don't tell me, Parker, a tall leggy blonde. Laurel mutters under her breath. Tempted to throw the letter away then, but something stops her, and she continues reading.

…like an auntie to me. You know the sort. The ones who want to kiss you and make everything better, even though they can't. Carrie is a tall leggy blonde…

Ha, I knew it!

… lesbian who wears the brightest red lipstick you could possibly buy. It really doesn't suit her, but she loves it.

Laurel re-reads the last couple of sentences several times before she exclaims. *Oh, Parker. How could I ever have doubted you?*

Anyway, that evening, seeing the state I was in, she encouraged me to speak to you. As you know it had been a while and we both had, and still have, punishing schedules. I didn't check myself in the mirror before we went to the restaurant. It wasn't until I saw myself on the camera that I realised how I looked. And what you would undoubtedly make of it. I often think back to the look on your face, and I can understand why you cut the call off. I don't blame you; I would have done the same, had the roles been reversed.

I'm sorry, Laurel. I should have tried harder to explain, and I should have told you how I was feeling. I'm so used to dealing with stuff myself, the emotions overwhelmed me, and I didn't know how to cope. Turning to the bottle is not the way I'll do it in the future. That night cost me the dearest thing to me. And that is you.

"Oh, Parker," Laurel calls into the air. "You silly thing."

Laurel finishes reading the letter, then picks up the photograph and turns it to face her. Tears of joy flow down her cheeks as she stares at the happy, laughing, joyous faces that smile back at her. The photo of her and Parker ice skating, just after he'd picked her up off the ice. Well, tried to until they both ended up in a heap on the floor, crying with laughter. Somehow Parker had managed to capture the perfect selfie of that moment.

Laurel dives out of her chair, almost knocking her second cup of cold tea to the floor and grabs her phone from her bag.

"Laurel, hi, how are you? I heard the album recording went swimmingly well."

"Yes, it did. It's given me an unexpected few days off, which I intend to enjoy, Brian. But do you know where Parker is staying?"

"Erm, well, yes, of course. Why?"

Brian knew things were tense between them, it was all Parker talked about.

"I really need to see him, but I want to surprise him. Oh, Brian, I got things so wrong."

Relief floods through Brian's veins. *Thank God.* He thinks, "Does that mean you're getting back together?"

"I don't know, Brian, but I'm going to try."

Sunday 2nd April 2023

Laurel has slept so well that she's shocked to discover that it's past 10am when she wakes. Brian has sent her Parker's hotel details, and she is surprised he is only staying a couple of streets away. She knows the hotel well, she waitressed there a few times when she was younger for pocket money. *It will be good to see the old place again.* She muses as she stretches before climbing out of bed and heading to the shower.

Drinking a cup of green tea (hot this time,) while she gets dressed. Casual but glamorous is the effect she is trying to achieve. After tying her hair in a loose ponytail, she smiles at the mirror. *Looking good girl. Even if I do say so myself.* She titters as she grabs her tiny, worn-out handbag from the kitchen table. *I must remember to buy myself a new bag.* She makes a mental note, as she locks the door behind her and sends Rash a text message telling him where she is headed. His 'right behind you, Miss,' response, reassures her. She trusts him implicitly. Especially now she's seen him in action.

Laurel arrives at the hotel and heads straight to the penthouse suite on the 10th floor. She guessed that's where he'd be, but Brian confirmed it last night. With a huge smile on her face, she knocks loudly on his door. Within seconds the door is flung open by a robed Parker.

"Laurel," He beams. "Come in. It's so good to see you. Full of cliché's this morning, aren't I? Sorry." He mumbles as nerves appear to take hold of him.

"Hi, Parker. Sorry to disturb you, I thought you'd be up and dressed by now. I wondered if you fancied grabbing some breakfast. My treat."

Parker stares into her piercing blue eyes. "I'd love to. Let me get dressed and we'll go."

Smiling, Laurel sits at the desk. Knowing if she sits on the bed, she'll end up in it and she wants to apologise to Parker over breakfast, not underneath the sheets.

Leading them to her favourite restaurant, Parker laughs. "Laurel. Why are you still eating here? You can afford to eat at the best restaurants in town now." He knows she's still getting used to this lifestyle, and he does like his posh restaurants.

"Because I like it here. The staff are warm and friendly, the place is cosy, and the food is basic but wonderful, why would I go elsewhere? Anyway, they need the custom to keep them going. They're a small family run business."

Parker acquiesces and follows her into the near empty tearoom. She sits at the back. Not wishing to air her washing in the openness of the window seating, the booth at the back is perfect. Parker glances around, taking it all in as Laurel orders them each a simple breakfast.

They make small talk while they await their food. Both comfortable in each other's company and in their surroundings. Parker is keen to know what's going through Laurel's mind. He's so desperate to give her the ring back. Ever the optimist, he'd snuck it into his pocket as they left his suite earlier.

Tucking into their breakfasts, Parker nods his head. "Mmm, Laurel, this is delicious. I can see why you want to keep coming here."

Swallowing her last mouthful, a smile of contentment spreads across her features. "Yes, I love it in here. I come here at least once a week when I'm home if I can. Although that will change as I get busier and tour again, I suppose. I like to support local businesses. They have all supported me in some small way and I want to see them thrive. Just like I am now."

Parker smiles at her. "You have such a wonderful heart, Laurel." He takes her hand and rubs his thumb over her knuckles and strokes her fingers. Laurel savours the sensation. She's missed his touch.

"Parker."

He looks up at her, still caressing her hand.

"I'm so sorry I misjudged you. And didn't give you chance to talk to me."

"It's okay, Laur…"

Laurel holds up her hand to silence him. "Please, Parker, let me say this."

He nods and she continues.

"I compared you to my past experiences. Which have mostly been bad, and seeing that lipstick took me back to a time I didn't want to revisit. Ever. A time when I came home early from work and caught my fiancé in bed with my then best friend. Cliché or what?" Laurel laughs as she takes a sip of her tea.

Parker doesn't speak so she continues.

"I thought we had it made. I thought that was my happy ever after. I was besotted with him. He was my everything. It took me a while to realise something was wrong. We were wrong for each other. I latched onto him in the hope that he would 'save' me. He would get me out of the rut I was in. When I found them together, I had the usual temper tantrum then I walked out. I had the clothes I stood up in and nothing else. I left it all. That was my signal to stand on my own two feet. Live my own life and rely on no one. That was a few years ago, and I've been single ever since. I've tried internet dating and dated a few times, but they all turned out to be a waste of time. When I saw that lipstick, I thought history was repeating itself. I'm so sorry, Parker."

"I guess we both learned a lesson. Or several, Laurel."

She nods. "Yes. Talk to each other and don't jump to conclusions."

"Absolutely."

"Thank you for the letter, Parker. Can we start again, please? I miss you so much. I feel I barely know you but also, I feel I've known you forever. It's strange."

"It isn't, Laurel. When we first met, I knew we would be together. I still hope for a very long time."

They kiss across the table and stare into each other's eyes. Parker takes the ring out of his pocket and slides it on her finger. "Marry me, Laurel."

Laurel nods. "Thank you for the second chance." She says. "Yes, yes, yes. I can't wait to be Mrs Small."

Parker grins. "Well, this is a first for me. I've never proposed to the same woman twice."

Laurel laughs. "I've never said yes to the same man twice either."

"Come on, let's go and celebrate." Parker says as he waits for her to take a couple of steps in front of him before he places a rather large tip on their table. Remembering what Laurel had said and how much he too had begun to fall in love with this quaint little tearoom. He'd be back.

Monday 3rd April 2023

"Kim. It's really you, come in." Laurel squeals as she answers the door to the incessant knocking. Laurel is expecting her best friend, but she's overslept. She is grateful that she has a few days before she starts her next tour. And even more grateful she still has her best friend to keep her grounded, she hugs Kim like she's hanging on for dear life.

As the friends hug, they both relax. Kim follows Laurel through to the kitchen as her friend makes them both a strong coffee.

"Come on then, Laurel, tell me everything."

Laurel barely knows where to begin it's been such a rollercoaster ride the past few months.

"It's wonderful, Kim." Laurel gushes, "but it's overwhelming, exhausting, exhilarating and everything in between. It's what I've always wanted, but it's taking some getting used to."

Kim smiles, she's always known Laurel had a famous singer in her bursting to get out. "I thought you would have moved by now."

Laurel sighs, "I did too, I just can't find the right place."

"Ah, you will, when the time is right. Maybe it's because you're going to move in with Parker." Kim's excitement for her friend is palpable.

Laurel gushes, "Ooh, wouldn't that be fantastic? I don't want to rush it though. Especially after…you know."

The girls have been in regular contact by text message but haven't seen each other since the comedy evening.

Kim nods her head. "Does his explanation ring true, Laurel?"

"Yes. My gut instinct tells me he's being honest, but you know I usually ignore it. I felt he was 'the one' when we first met, but how many times have I said that?"

Kim laughs, "More times than you've had hot dinners!"

Laurel laughs too, "I'd be lost without you, Kim. Thank you for being my friend."

Kim hugs her again and they settle into catching up with each other's lives since they last met.

"And, Laurel." Kim, hands on hips, stares out of the window. "Who is that man loitering in the rather understated BMW across the street?"

Laurel looks over her friend's shoulder, "Ah, that's Rash. My… bodyguard."

Kim laughs, "Check you out Whitney Houston."

"I wish," Laurel answers. "Well actually, I don't.

He was foisted on me when I left Scotland but he's great. He's rather dishy, to be honest. You'd like him."

"Mmm," Kim mutters as she watches him from behind the curtain. He hasn't taken his eyes off Laurel's building, and she can see his phone balancing on the dashboard.

"I'll introduce you. Let me get changed and we can go for a walk. I need some fresh air."

As they make their way to Rash's car, Kim can see his gorgeous face through the open window.

"Is everything alright, Miss?" Rash asks Laurel as she stops and leans against the sparkling black paintwork. "Everything is great, thank you, Rash. How about you?"

Rash likes his new charge. She's everything all the other stars he's worked with aren't. She's kind, funny, caring, and he feels very protective of her.

"I'm good, thank you, Miss. Glad you're okay too."

"Rash, this is my best friend, Kim."

"Ah, the lady who made you enter Mr Parker's competition." Rash grins.

"That's the one. I wanted to introduce you, being as you're both going to be a big part of my life."

Rash climbs out of the car to shake Kim's hand.

Oh, my goodness, I think I'm in love. She gasps as she accepts Rash's hand.

"Pleased to meet you, Miss Kim."

"Likewise." Is all she can mutter.

Giggling to herself, Laurel takes over. "Rash, we're going for a walk. Care to join us?"

"Oh, Miss, that would be lovely, but I must remain unobtrusive in order to protect you both."

Disappointed, but understanding his situation, Laurel simply nods in acknowledgement, grabs Kim's hand, and begins to walk towards the park. She doesn't need to look around to know that Rash isn't far behind.

"Oh, my word, Laurel, you weren't kidding, he is a dish."

Laurel laughs, as she links her arm through Kim's as they meander around the park. "This is so nice, Kim, thank you so much for coming. I really needed to do something… normal today."

"Laurel, your…normal… is so much different to how it was. You need to get used to it. I'm amazed there are no prying reporters waiting to leap out at us."

"I know, Kim. I'm getting used to it, but everything seemed to happen all at once. I am living my best life and I'm so grateful I still have you to keep me sane."

"You will always have me, Lol. I'm always here."

"Likewise." Laurel confirms. "The reporters gave up in the end, although they never really bothered me. They can't get close with Rash and the rest of the gang always on high alert. It feels good to be honest. I finally feel like…me."

Kim hugs her friend, pleased at last that she's found herself. "Now, Lol, tell me all about this handsome devil walking behind us."

"Oh, no, I'm not doing your dirty work. You can get to know him yourself. You're not backwards in coming forwards, ask him out on a date. I dare you."

"What! Are you kidding me, I can't do that."

"Of course you can, Kim." Laurel ticks off on her fingers all the reason's she should ask Rash out. "A) because you can. B) because it's you. You are the most confident person I know. C) because it's the 21st century and anything goes, basically. D) because I'm not doing it for you, this time."

Kim squirms remembering the last time Laurel fixed her up on a blind date. "Okay, okay, you win. I'll ask him when we get back."

Laurel grins from ear to ear. "His next day off is Thursday and as you're off for the Easter holidays next week, you can have a day date."

"Oh, you have it all worked out, don't you, Miss Laurel." Kim retorts.

"Yep. It's going to be fabulous."

True to her word as soon as Kim leaves Laurel's later that day, she wanders over to Rash, sat where he was when she first spotted him a few hours ago, and asks him out. Amazed when he says yes, Kim can't help but do a little happy dance as she rounds the corner to her car. She is already planning in her head what she's going to wear for her date.

Laurel watches from the window as her friend walks away from Rash, certain from her body language that she's landed herself a date. *I'm good at this matchmaking lark.* Laurel laughs to herself as she settles down in front of the TV with a cup of green tea and a healthy protein snack. She's glad she's had the time with her friend, it's going to be months before she sees her again. She's also glad she's able to have some 'me' time. Once she's finished her cuppa she heads to the bathroom and luxuriates in a steaming hot bath. Allowing her body to relax and her mind to wonder, she falls into a dreamy sleep.

Woken by an intense chill, Laurel shivers and takes a moment to work out where she is. The water is so cold it's hurting her bones. Grabbing the towel from the rail in front of her, she dries herself quickly, wraps herself in her fluffy white dressing gown, and slides her feet into her bright pink slippers. Heading for the kitchen she glances at the time on the DVD player. *I've only been in the bath half an hour; how come I feel like I've slept the sleep of the dead?* Shaking herself awake she makes herself a cup of strong black coffee. Unusual for her, but the weird dream she just had has shocked her to the core. Not usually one for overreacting, she grabs her mobile and makes a call.

"Hey, Laurel, what's up?"

"Erm, Brian, I… Oh, I don't know."

"Laurel, you're stuttering, what's wrong, are you safe?" Brian senses something in Laurel's voice he's never heard in her before. Fear. But he isn't sure why. He knows she's safe, he checks in with Rash as often as he can.

"Yes, yes, I'm fine. I'm safe. Rash is outside. It's… It's…ridiculous, I've just had the weirdest dream, but it felt so real. Like I was experiencing it there and then."

Brian breathes a sigh of relief and forces his heart to stop racing. "Oh, Laurel, you had me so worried then."

"I'm sorry, Brian, I didn't know who else to call."

"Why didn't you call Parker?"

"Well, I couldn't. He'll be on stage now and, the dream was about him." Not wanting to beat around the bush and desperate to know the truth, Laurel didn't think or even care that she was asking his brother this. "Brian, is Parker cheating on me?"

"Erm." Brian takes a breath. Used to his brothers' ways he wasn't surprised by the question. He was annoyed though, he thought Parker had found 'the one.'

"I'm sorry, Brian, I shouldn't have asked. This puts you in an awkward position. Forget I called." Flustered more than anything, Laurel's finger hovers over the 'end call' button when she hears Brian call her name.

"Laurel. He has a track record, but I thought he was settled with you. What makes you think he's cheating? Is it just the dream?"

Crossing his fingers, Brian waits for her response.

"No. Brian. There are so many other 'little' things I've noticed. One instance on a video call he had lipstick on the side of his mouth. He passed it off as an overzealous lesbian aunt in the form of his PA."

Laurel thought she heard an agonised cry from the other end of the phone. "Brian. Are you okay?"

"Laurel, you really need to speak to Parker. He'll be off stage in half an hour. I'll make sure he video calls you."

"I can't… I don't want…This could ruin everything, Brian."

"Why, Laurel, you have to do what's right for you, and you have to know. If he is cheating, you're better off without him."

"I know Brian, but he's your brother and you're my manager. It will all fall apart." *Just when everything was finally working in my favour.*

"Laurel, I'll always be here as your manager and your friend, no matter what happens between you and Parker."

"Blood is thicker than water, Brian."

"Not in this case, Laurel. There is so much you don't know, and it's best kept that way. Let me know how it goes with Parker later."

Laurel puts her phone on the table next to her and tucks her feet under herself on the sofa. Sipping the now cooling coffee, she grabs her notebook and pen and begins writing her dream down. She wishes she hadn't called Brian. He'll probably spill his guts to Parker and her world will fall apart, but Brian's right, she needs to know.

Monday 3rd April – Midnight

"This is a nice surprise, Laurel, I didn't think we would get chance to speak until next week, but Brian said I should call you. It's so good to see your face. You look gorgeous in that fluffy white robe." Parker gushes. "I wish…"

Laurel couldn't help but wonder whether Brian had said anything, or whether Parker was just... being Parker.

Not wanting to beat around the bush. She's feeling exhausted from the power the dream seems to have over her, Laurel stops him in his tracks. Putting her hand up to the camera, she barks, "Enough, already, Parker."

"What's wrong, Laurel?" Parker moves closer to the camera, looking for signs on her face and in her eyes that something is wrong.

"Are you cheating on me?" Laurel too moves closer to the camera. Had they been face to face she would have been staring into his eyes for any obvious signs. She's heard of whirlwind romances that last decades, but now she doesn't feel like this is going to be one of them.

Stunned into silence, Parker stutters. "Wha…Why…Who…"

"So, the answer is yes, then is it, Parker?"

"Where did this come from, Laurel? Who's been spreading rumours?" Parker can feel his blood pressure rising, but he has to keep calm.

"Parker. There are so many little inconsistencies it's impossible not to imagine. Plus, the dream I had earlier was so vivid, I could almost have been watching you and Carrie get it on in your hotel suite." Keeping calm, Laurel continues. "Carrie is not a leggy blond lesbian at all, is

163

she, Parker?" Laurel could feel her anger rising but she knew that would get her nowhere.

Parker shook his head from side to side and covered his face with his hands.

"No, she isn't."

"I think that's enough talk, Parker. Thank you for everything, but it really is over now."

Laurel clicks the leave meeting button and sits for a while staring at the wall in front of her. She feels surprisingly calm. Almost serene. Feelings she wouldn't usually associate with a breakup. Maybe she's finally learning to value herself in all her relationships.

Sending a quick message to Brian, '*It's over with Parker. Speak to you tomorrow. Thank you for being there.*'

Leaving her phone on the table, Laurel grabs a glass of water from the kitchen and heads to bed. This time, the dream is much more pleasing.

On Tour

Before her next tour begins, Laurel puts her flat on the market. She instructs agents and solicitors to do whatever it is they need to do to sell it. She has nowhere to go when she gets home but it feels good to finally be letting go of the old place.

"Are you sure you're doing the right thing with the flat?" Brian asks as they enter his suite to discuss this afternoon's show.

The tour is exceeding their expectations and Laurel is having such a good time. The minor day to day things like selling her flat, not having anywhere to move to when she gets back, and the dross the media is apparently spouting about her don't even register on her to do list. In fact. She no longer has one of those. Her belief in herself and a lot of luck have got her to where she is today. She isn't overthinking it; she's enjoying it. For the first time in her life. And it feels good.

"Yes, Bri, I'm sure. I've clung on to so many things for so long. And people in the past and it hasn't served me well. I can rent for a while or stay in a hotel if I need to, but I'm not sure what will happen after the tour."

"But." Brian has so many questions. This once shy girl is on top of her game, and he worries about her. He cares about her more than anyone else in his life, which surprises him. If only he could tell her.

Laurel who has been doing 10 minutes of stretching and breathing exercises to relax herself after being on stage, stops halfway through a cat-cow pose and looks up at him.

For the first time since she's met him, she actually looks at him. She feels like she's staring but she isn't. *I'm looking into his soul.* Surprised by the emotions which surge through her body, she is taken aback. She's never looked at Brian in a sexual way. She saved that for his errant brother, but the feelings in her heart, soul, and gut, are feelings she's never had before. *Is this love? Is this what love feels like?* She is hit by these sudden thoughts, and they take her breath away. Curling herself into the child's pose position to stretch her back and avert her gaze, she gives a somewhat muffled response.

"It's good. I finally feel like I'm me. I don't need to worry about where I'm going to live, or who with, or anything else, really. I'm learning to live in the moment and the decision to sell the flat just felt… right. Does that make sense?"

As she uncurls from her pose, Laurel sits up and looks into Brian's eyes. *Say it, Laurel, say it.*

"I worry about you, Laurel." Brian says before she can open her mouth. "I know the split with Parker must have affected you, although you never say anything."

Even though they are brothers, and they are close, this is the first time Brian has mentioned Parker, and they are already 6 weeks into the tour. Brian has been flitting between destinations and is still managing both of their careers.

Laurel sighs. "Brian, he drives me mad. He texts all the time and calls virtually daily now, but I'm not interested. I've moved on and he needs to as well."

"Have you, though?"

"Yes, I really have. I'm grateful to him as I've learned so much about myself in the last few months and a lot of it is thanks to Parker. I have told him he can have my friendship but nothing else. I love him, but in a different way to how I thought I did."

Brian looks at her. He thought he understood as his feelings for this girl were growing daily. He has always had relationships with men. His relationship with Laurel, although not sexual, feels deeper than anything he's ever experienced before.

As if reading his mind, Laurel echoes his thoughts. As they look into each other's eyes the words roll off their tongues in unison.

"I love you, Laurel."

"I love you, Brian."

A knock on the door breaks the spell. Brian dives for the door handle as Laurel grabs her bag and coat, ready to make a quick exit.

Fumbling around for the key to her hotel room door, Laurel beats a hasty retreat and leaves Brian discussing business with his PA. Stumbling into her room she throws her bag on the desk in the corner and flops onto the bed. *What the hell just happened?* Lying on her back, Laurel stares at the ornately patterned ceiling. A feeling of complete calm washes over her. A feeling she hasn't experienced before after declaring her undying love for someone. *Is this how it's supposed to be?* She ponders to herself as she relives those last few moments in Brian's suite. Her heart, soul and body are screaming yes at her. A big smile forms across her face, so big, it lights up her eyes. Pulling herself off the bed, she moves to the bathroom and stares at herself in the mirror. *Wow. Girl. You look good.* Her eyes don't usually sparkle like this, but she feels different, somehow. Grabbing a bottle of water from the not-so-mini, mini bar, she picks up her notebook and pen, and sits down at the oak desk and begins to write down how she's feeling. The buzz is incredible. She can't quite explain it. She doesn't need to. The notebook understands. She is so engrossed in writing; she almost misses the gentle tap on the door. It isn't until she hears his soothing voice call her name that she realises Brian is outside her room. Dashing across the room she flings the door open.

"Laurel."

"Brian."

They both whisper each other's names, breathless as they fall into a tight embrace. Edging their way back into the room, Brian kicks the door closed behind him. He does not want to let this woman go. Ever.

Eventually breaking their hug, they sit on the king-sized bed, holding hands, staring into each other's eyes. She is the first to break the companionable silence.

"Bri, what's happening to us?"

Brian shakes his head. "I don't know. I've never felt like this before."

"Me neither," Laurel admits, "what are we going to do?"

"Make love until the sun rises?" Brian asks.

"We can't. What about Stef? And. By the way, I thought you were gay?"

"I'm having trouble computing this in my brain, but I think I know what's happening." Brian says, still holding her hand. He stares into her eyes, losing himself there for a moment. Before breaking eye contact, he releases her hand, and stands up, walking over to the window to gaze at the beautiful sunset.

"Come and look at this, Laurel." He calls over his shoulder.

She rises and stands by his side.

"This is what life is all about," he begins, "sharing moments like this with special people."

Laurel nods. She cannot find her voice, unusual for a singer, but she's so enraptured in the moment, that nothing else matters.

The sun sets behind the castle a couple of minutes later and they turn to look at each other. Brian continues to tell her what he feels is happening.

"Laurel. I think we've just found the love we have both been seeking for many years."

Laurel quietly agrees.

"It's strange. Stef is the only person to have shown me any compassion, and what I thought was love. It just never felt like this. No expectations or rules. Just. Love. I've been chasing what I thought was love all my life, when just being myself, has brought it to me, in the strangest of ways. Does this make any sense to you, Laurel?"

"Yes," Laurel answers, her throat constricting with emotion. "Yes, it does. I feel the same. It was such a gentle, unassuming, calm tug at my heartstrings, in that moment, and I just…knew. I now realise that all my previous relationships, including your brother, have been about attachment, externalising, and sexual gratification. I now feel the unconditional love I was truly searching for all these years."

Brian pulls her to him, "I couldn't have put it better myself."

His eyes look into hers and his mouth seeks her mouth. The most tender kiss ensues, sending the gentlest of tingles down her spine. Brian, like his brother, is tall and muscular. His piercing green eyes bore into hers as his shovel-like hands pull her further into him. Their breath and heartbeats sync in perfect harmony as he picks her up

169

and carries her to the bed. Placing her gently on top of the covers he drinks her in. She is glowing and he is in love. Although they have never touched before, he feels like he knows every inch of her body. Her long red hair spills over the pillow. Leaning into her he takes her glasses off.

Her breath catches. *How can I find that sexy.* Laurel muses as she savours every movement Brian makes.

Placing her glasses on the bedside cabinet, he plants a kiss on both of her eyelids, both of her cheeks and her mouth. Unzipping the bright pink designer hoodie, he exposes her pert breasts. *Wow.* He exclaims as he straddles her and pulls her light grey jogging bottoms off, discarding them on the floor beside the bed. Still fully clothed in dark blue suit trousers with a pristine white shirt, unbuttoned to his navel, exposing light grey hairs, Brian takes her left nipple in his mouth and gently sucks. Tickling her very erect nipples with the end of his tongue. Laurel arches her back. Her body tingles under his touch. Still straddling her, he works his way down every inch of her body until she feels ready to burst. Her hands find their way to his shirt, and she undoes the remaining buttons and discards the shirt with her clothes on the floor. Their heartbeats are synced. Laurel sits up and kisses every inch of his chest, sucking his nipples as she passes them. His erection very apparent through his trousers. Although Brian is strong, Laurel catches him unawares and rolls him over until he's lay on his back. Slowly undoing his trousers, she is surprised that he is commando. *Wow.* She bites her lip in anticipation. Knowing what she is about to experience will be different to anything she's had before. Taking his trousers off and adding them to the pile, she slides down his body and lies by his side. Her head rests on her right hand as her left hand caresses his muscular

170

torso, thighs, and legs. It's her turn to drink him in. Her fingers tug gently at his pubic hair. He purrs.

"Laurel." He whispers.

"Brian."

She manoeuvres her body on top of his, her eyes, don't leave his.

They kiss. In one deft movement she slides herself down his erection. They both gasp as he enters her. They fit together so perfectly. Moving in rhythm to their heartbeats the passion heightens, and they make love like neither of them has ever done before. It's almost as if their souls are making love too. Slowly she rides him to an all-engulfing crescendo. As they let themselves go, they climax together, whispering each other's names.

Lying side by side, big grins on both of their faces, Laurel breaks the sensual silence. "What happens now then? What about Stef?"

Brian takes a deep breath. "Stef and I were over a long time ago."

Laurel turns to face him. She's heard that line so many times in the past, but this time it feels like it is true.

"Really, when?" Laurel can't help but ask.

"Just after Christmas."

Laurel is shocked. "But it's April now, how come you never said anything?"

"I didn't know what to say, or how to say it, to be honest."

Thinking about it, Laurel hadn't seen Stef around for a long time, she assumed he was working.

Laurel has so many questions, and so does Brian, but it's late and they have a busy day tomorrow. They snuggle into each other's arms and have the best night's sleep either of them has had in a very long time.

171

The next morning, they rise early. There are still a few weeks left of the tour which gives them time to get used to their changed situation and work out how they're going to tell everyone.

Walking towards the venue for this evening's show, Laurel asks, "what went wrong with you and Stef? You looked so happy together." To Laurel they always looked like the perfect couple, so happy and always laughing and smiling.

"He saw the way I looked at you."

"What!" Laurel exclaims. "What... When…What do you mean?"

"As soon as Parker introduced us, I knew I wanted to be with you. I was so happy when you finally dumped him. He's my brother, but he's a tit most of the time."

Laurel laughs at the apt description of her ex-lover. "He's lovely. In his own way. He has a heart of gold but he's... I don't know, confused, guilty, angry." Laurel says. Although they aren't together anymore, she still feels something towards Parker. He's helped change her life, after all.

"I think he's all those things, Laurel and I don't know how to help him. This...us...won't do him much good but we have to get on with our lives."

"You're right, Bri, we'll tell everyone as soon as we get home."

The rest of the tour goes off without incident. Laurel has the best time of her life. Her emotions apparent through her singing. Pinching herself occasionally to make sure it is really her on that stage she begins to enjoy her other dream come true.

Final Day of Tour

"Ready, Laurel?" Brian asks as they stand in the wings while the service announcements play over the speakers. The usual 'no video, no photography etc...' no one takes any notice of. The team have already shown her pirate videos on social media. Laurel doesn't care. She loves what she does, and she doesn't look at her social media profiles anymore. Her team do all the PR, she just sings. The way she's always wanted it to be.

"Ready," Laurel confirms. As she takes her first step onto the stage she sees Parker, Stef, Rash, and Kim in the front row of the 20,000-seater stadium. Thrown for a minute she stands and stares, looking back into the wings she sees Brian with his thumbs up, egging her on.

"Go get 'em, Girl." He's mouthing to her.

The final show sees two encores and Laurel doesn't want the evening to end. She's exhausted but exhilarated. After the last number, her now infamous *Love Is*, is reprised, (now number one in the UK and Australian charts,) Brian walks on stage.

"Good evening, everyone," Brian calls for the audience to be calm as he has an announcement. The entire room holds its breath. Everyone is assuming that he's going to say their idol isn't touring again, or worse that she's ill. He says none of those things. Walking to the front of the stage, he takes her left hand in his and slowly drops onto his right knee. "Laurel Sage Rivers, will you do me the great honour of becoming my wife?"

A cheer loud enough to take off the roof of the building erupts. When the room has calmed again, Laurel looks deep into Brian's soul and simply says. "Yes."

The crowd erupts again, and nothing will stop the reporters and photographers now. Out of the corner of her eye, she sees her friend, Kim, and her security manager Rash, embrace and kiss. Her heart swells. Turning, she sees Parker, hand in hand with Stef, a look of adoration on his face. He catches her eye and winks. It appears they all have a lot of catching up to do. But for now, she turns her attention back to Brian, and loses herself in his kiss.

The End

About the Author

Hi, I'm Lisa. I hope you enjoyed reading this romance novella. If you did, please leave me a review, or send me some feedback.

Here's a bit about me.

I am an author, inspirational speaker, and intuitive.

In 2020, I wrote my debut novel, Katie, A New Chapter, a self-help work of fiction based on my life experiences. I touch on mental health, abuse, and trauma in my story.

Working recently in a prison I have seen many breakthroughs with the men. I am also proud to say the book has helped to save a life.

I love writing both for enjoyment and to facilitate the healing process for myself and others and often use writing to help channel spiritual messages. My second novel, Tom, The Next Chapter was published in 2022, and this, my first romance novella, in 2024.

As an inspirational speaker, I openly share my story and speak on topics including:

*Being your authentic self,

*Building your confidence, and,

*Developing good mental wellbeing.

My talks are interactive so make sure you have a pen and a piece of paper.

Very often, it only requires a small change to make all the difference in your life. I'm here to help you change the areas you feel stuck in or are struggling with. Often a change in one area has a lasting impact on all the other areas of your life: career, health, wealth, and relationships.

In my spare time, I love to sing, walk, and read.

You can contact me at lisa@lisambillingham.com or via my website: www.lisambillingham.com

Other titles written by Lisa:

Never Look Back Series
Book 1 - Katie, A New Chapter (2020)
Book 2 - Tom, The Next Chapter (2022)

Acknowledgements & Contacts

With thanks to:

Carol McIntyre and Lynne Thomas for being my guinea pigs and giving me pre-publication feedback. Simon Mansel for his help with the fire research.

Here are a few professional contacts I worked with to produce this book.

My friend, VA, and avid reader - Carol McIntyre carol@exec-pro-va.com

My friend & social media marketing expert, Lynne Thomas - info@thebusinessbuilderonline.com

Cover design by
Chris Thomas – Chris@thebusinessbuilderonline.com

Printed in Great Britain
by Amazon

39377762R00108